no secrets

The Story of a Girl Band

Sneaking Around

2

By Nancy Krulik

GROSSET & DUNLAP • NEW YORK

For Mandy

Text copyright © 2001 by Nancy Krulik. Cover and insert photographs
copyright © 2001 by David Croland. All rights reserved. Published by
Grosset & Dunlap, a division of Penguin Putnam Books for Young Readers,
New York. GROSSET & DUNLAP is a trademark of Penguin Putnam Inc.
Published simultaneously in Canada. Printed in the USA.

ISBN 0-448-42581-5   A B C D E F G H I J

Chapter 1

Despite the relentlessly cold November wind, Melanie Sun stood outside, just staring at the brownstone that was about to become her new home. To anyone walking by, the four-story building with the winding cement stairway might have looked like any of the other landmark buildings on West Eightieth Street. But Melanie knew better. There was true star-making magic within the walls of that one hundred-year-old house on Manhattan's Upper West Side.

Melanie felt a drip of water fall on her head. The sky had been threatening to rain all day, and now it was finally coming down. Quickly, Mel picked up the case that housed her electric keyboard, darted up the stairs, and opened the door—to the building *and* to her future.

A tall, thin, twenty-something-year-old woman with thick blond hair greeted Melanie in the front hallway. "Hi, Melanie, I'm Candace," she introduced herself. "I'll be your voice coach, dorm supervisor, and all-around confidante."

Melanie put down her keyboard, forced a nervous smile to her lips, and held out her hand. "Pleased to meet you," she said, trying her best to be polite. "I'm sorry I'm so late, but I had trouble with the trains—you know how that can be."

Candace nodded. "Getting into Manhattan can be a real drag," she agreed. "But your aunt called ahead to say you'd be late. It was smart of you to tell her to do that. Shows responsibility. Eileen likes that."

Melanie's smile was genuine now. The "Eileen" Candace had mentioned was actually Eileen Kerr, the head of Omega Talent. Just a few weeks ago Eileen had come to the Professional Children's Boarding School in search of girls to be part of her latest creation, a pop music group called No Secrets. Eileen and her staff had spent a few days walking around the boarding school, observing the 150 students as they danced, sang, and interacted with one another. Then Eileen had chosen eight girls to move into the Omega brownstone on West Eightieth Street and train intensely for life as a pop star. Melanie had been one of the lucky eight.

But Melanie knew that didn't mean that she'd definitely made No Secrets. In fact, only four of the girls would wind up being part of the actual band. Still, Melanie was thrilled to be one of the eight semifinalists handpicked by Eileen Kerr. She was surprised, too, since most of the Omega Talent bands were filled with sweet, blond-haired, blue-eyed girls from the west coast. Melanie was none of those things. Born and bred in one the tougher areas of Brooklyn, Mel was Chinese, with long, straight black hair that was often more tousled than tamed. She had a rose tattoo on her ankle and a pierced belly button. None of the Omega girls up till now could boast that.

"Your room is on the third floor, first door to your left. Your roommate is already there," Candace informed Melanie.

"Who'm I rooming with?" Melanie asked her.

"We put you with Serena Barkin. She didn't go home for the Thanksgiving holiday, so she was able to get here first thing this morning. She got to pick her side of the room before you got here. But I'm sure you girls will be able to work that out."

Melanie shrugged. "Whatever. Before I moved to PCBS I was living in a two-bedroom apartment with three cousins and my aunt. Having just *one* roommate seems like heaven—no matter which side of the room I crash on."

Candace laughed. "Great! Your bags are already up there. Why don't you go and unpack? You'll want to get to bed early tonight—Eileen has scheduled a meeting for seven thirty tomorrow morning. Breakfast is at six forty-five."

Melanie tried to keep the shock from registering on her face. She'd never dreamed that Eileen Kerr expected her girl groups to be morning people. Melanie had always thought of musicians as night owls, who worked all night and did most of their sleeping while the "suits" of the world were at their offices.

But she didn't want to seem like a troublemaker right from the start. "Gotcha!" she said as she raced up to the third floor.

The door to Melanie's room was slightly ajar when she got there. She forced the door open and walked in. Serena was sitting on one bed, so completely focused on taping a poster onto the wall that she didn't even notice Melanie. Without disturbing her new roommate's concentration, Melanie plopped her bag on top of the other bed and kicked off her shoes. She watched as Serena made sure the poster was hanging straight and then put the tape in place. The picture was of two little babies—a boy and a girl—alone on a beach. Typical Serena, Melanie thought to herself. The girl was just a sweet little Iowa innocent with a love of all things cute and cuddly.

"What's that?" Melanie moaned, pointing to the poster.

"Well, hello to you, too," Serena greeted her with a grin. "Do you like the poster? I bought it at some photo store on Columbus Avenue yesterday."

"It's fine," Melanie said, sighing. "But do you think you could move it to another wall? It's just not the first thing I want to see when I walk into the room."

Serena shrugged and wiped a wisp of her soft red hair from her forehead. Then she carefully removed the tape from the corners and moved the soft-focus black-and-white poster to her closet door.

"Thanks, Serena," Melanie said. Then she reached into her bag and pulled out a poster that featured a one-eyed, creepy rag doll propped up against a wall. She taped the poster to her closet door.

"Oooh. What's that?" Serena asked squeamishly.

"KoRn's first album cover. Isn't it cool?" Melanie asked her. "I bring it everywhere with me. Once I put it on the wall, I know I'm home."

Serena looked at the two posters, which were taped side by side on adjoining closet doors. The posters said a lot about the two girls who shared the room. "This arrangement is certainly going to be interesting," she mused.

Melanie laughed. It was true. No two girls could be more different than her and Serena. "Hey look, it won't be so bad," she assured her new roomie. "At least neither of us is rooming with Daria. I wonder who got stuck with her?"

The phone rang loudly in Daria and Katie's room. "Can you get that?" Katie asked in her distinctive Texas drawl. "I'm in the middle of ironing this blouse."

"You get it," Daria moaned as she placed a few pearl hair clips in her long brown hair. "It's bound to be Keith again. After all, he's only called twice in the past half hour."

Katie sighed as she turned off the iron and stood it on its end. Then she reached over and pulled the portable phone from its base. "Hello?" she greeted the caller. Then a smile formed on her face. Her blond ponytail bopped up and down with excitement. "Daddy! Oh, I miss you and Mom already! Yes, of course I'm fine. The plane got in about an hour ago. We weren't very late at all. I just found the picture of Cornflower you slipped into my suitcase. She's just the most beautiful horse in the world!"

Daria rolled her eyes as she heard Katie chatter away with her father. It seemed to Daria that her new roommate had been on the phone all day long. She'd already spoken twice to her boyfriend, Keith, and both times she'd been depressed when she'd hung up. Keith definitely did not like the idea of having his "sugar" living all the way up north in New York City.

Katie was babbling on and on about the dinner on the plane, and the passengers who were sitting around her. Daria rolled her eyes. From the looks of things, Katie would be on the phone with her dad for a while now.

Not that Daria was expecting any phone calls. Her parents had hardly ever called her during the two years she'd been at PCBS, and she didn't expect them to start now. It wasn't that the Griffiths didn't care about their only child; it was just that they were incredibly busy running their own law firm. The "family business," as Daria's mother liked to call the firm, took up most of their time. In fact, one of Daria's mother's personal assistants had been the one to drive Daria to O'Hare Airport that very morning. Her parents had had a benefit breakfast to attend, and they couldn't change their plans in time to give their only child a lift to the plane.

Daria put on her Walkman and let the sound of

Nine Inch Nails drown out Katie's incessant giggling. Even before she'd moved into the brownstone, Daria had promised Eileen Kerr that she would be a team player when it came to trying out for No Secrets. But as she listened to Katie go on and on, that suddenly seemed easier said than done.

Alyssa Wilkinson knocked hard on her friend Janine Gutierrez's second-floor room in the brownstone. She wanted to make sure Janine could hear her over the loud Santana CD that was currently blaring from the stereo.

"Come in," Janine replied, turning down the sound.

"Wanna go get a slice, Janine?" Alyssa asked as she walked into the room. She looked around for Janine's roommate. "What happened to Cass?"

"Oh, she had to go off and meet some music industry type that her mother wanted her to get to know," Janine replied.

Alyssa sighed. Cassidy Sanders's mother was truly incredible—in her own, possessive way. Even though she lived all the way in California, she still managed to find a way to control her daughter's every move. She'd been doing that for years—both as Cass's parent and as her manager.

Cass was the only one of the eight finalists who'd ever worked professionally. She'd had her first shot at stardom as the lead in the TV show *The Kids Company*. The program had been the number one kid's show in America, and Cass's face had been plastered on the cover of hundreds of magazines. She and her mother went to movie premieres and traveled all over the world. But that was then. *The Kids Company* had been canceled two years ago, and Cass's career sort of ended. Cass had opted to come and study music, dance, and acting in New York, and Alana had stayed behind in Los Angeles.

It was pretty obvious to Cass's friends that it was Alana who really missed the spotlight. In fact, when the eight semifinalists for No Secrets had been announced, it was hard to tell who was more excited—Cass or her mom.

Alyssa was pretty sure that a girl with Cass's striking looks, bouncy brown hair, and stick-thin figure would get another shot at stardom, eventually. But Alyssa also knew that Alana Morgan was not the type of woman to just bide her time waiting for the next big break. So it was pretty much a given that Alana would be visiting New York again real soon. She wasn't about to leave Cass's new shot at stardom to chance.

"Oh well, Cass wouldn't have wanted to have pizza, anyway," Janine told Alyssa. "You know she hardly ever eats after eight o'clock. She says that's when the pounds go on. I sure wish I had her willpower." Janine looked down at her own legs and quickly untucked her shirt from her jeans. "I think this looks better, huh, 'Lyss?" she asked. "At least it covers my butt."

Alyssa shook her head. "There's nothing wrong

with your butt. There's only something wrong with your head. You're obsessed with your figure. Frankly, I wouldn't want to look like Cass. She's too thin."

Janine began to brush her short brown hair. "Well, you have to admit there aren't too many full-figured girls in Eileen Kerr's other groups," she reminded Alyssa.

"There aren't too many African-American girls with eggplant-colored hair, either," Alyssa countered, running her fingers through her head of purple highlights. "But I'm here. I think Eileen is going for a different kind of look this time around."

Janine smiled. "Considering the combo of girls now living at this brownstone, I'd say that was a pretty solid guess." She straightened the pile of notebooks on her desk. "Do you think Eileen is gonna give us a break on some of this schoolwork? It's gonna be tough keeping up with studying while we're learning to be a band."

"You heard what Ms. Geoffries told us before we left PCBS to come to the brownstone," Alyssa reminded Janine. She lowered her voice to sound like the authoritative, chain-smoking headmistress. "'You girls are still members of the Professional Children's Boarding School, and will be held to the same academic standards as our other students.'"

Alyssa grinned as Janine exploded with laughter at her dead-on impersonation.

"Well, I already wrote an entry in my self-expression journal for English class," Janine told

9

Alyssa. "That's one requirement I don't mind keeping up with."

Alyssa sighed. Writing down her feelings came easily to Janine. Alyssa was more geared toward keeping those things inside. That journal was a total thorn in Alyssa's side.

"Wanna ask Hannah to come with us?" Janine asked, interrupting Alyssa's thoughts.

Alyssa bristled at the mention of her roommate. "You want to ask Hannah Linden, New York debutante, to do something as pedestrian as hop across the street to a local pizza parlor? I don't think the ambience is quite her style. There are no roaming violins or crystal chandeliers."

Janine laughed. "She's not really all that bad. She's just sort of quiet. I think maybe she's shy."

Alyssa shot Janine a glance and frowned doubtfully. Janine had to be kidding. Hannah'd never made a single attempt to befriend any of the girls at PCBS—preferring instead to meet up with her Park Avenue chums whenever possible. At least that's what Alyssa assumed she did. Hannah wasn't too forthcoming about her free-time plans. Or about anything else, for that matter. While the girls at PCBS had discovered a lot about each other's lives, nobody knew anything about Hannah, except that she always wore classic, but chic, designer clothing, and that her long, dark brown hair was impeccably styled. Totally superficial stuff.

"Okay, so maybe she hasn't exactly expressed a

desire to be friends," Janine admitted begrudgingly. "But we're all going to have to live here together, and we're all going to have to get along. We don't want anyone to feel left out—that kind of bad feeling will throw us all off."

Alyssa didn't say anything. More than anyone else in the brownstone, she knew what it was like to feel left out. Alyssa's dad was in the army. Her whole life was one series of moves after another as her family followed her dad as he got transferred to different bases around the country. They never stayed in one place for very long, and Alyssa always seemed to be the new girl—the one who never had a lab partner, a locker companion, or even a really good friend to gossip with during lunch.

But life at PCBS had been different for Alyssa. She'd lived at the school for three years—longer than she'd been anywhere else. She finally knew what it was like to be part of a crowd. Maybe Janine was right: Perhaps inviting Hannah to come along once in a while was the right thing to do.

Just not tonight.

"Okay, Janine, you win," Alyssa said finally. "Tomorrow we ask Hannah to hang with us. Heck, I'll even ask Daria to join us."

Janine bristled. "Well, let's not go too crazy about this," she interrupted.

Alyssa laughed. "Look, this is our last night of freedom before Eileen Kerr has us working our butts off. So tonight I say we scarf down some pizza, gossip, and just hang out together."

Janine smiled at her best friend. "You're on," she agreed. "As long as we can order a few slices with pepperoni."

Okay, here I am, back in New York City. It was so great hanging with Janine tonight. I am so glad we were both asked to move into the brownstone. She's the first best friend I've ever had. It would've really been awful for one of us to have been left downtown at the PCBS dorms while the other was here at the Omega brownstone.

Of course, the two of us being here means we're in competition with each other for one of those four No Secrets spots. But I'm trying not to look at it that way. I just want both of us to make the group. I want that more than anything.

My mom knows exactly how I feel. She gave me a new charm for my bracelet before I left—a four-leaf clover that she hoped would bring me luck. It's great to know she believes in me.

I just wish my dad had the same faith. I think he's glad for me and all that, but he's also afraid that I won't make the group and that I'll be crushed or something. When I told him that I wouldn't even entertain the idea that I won't be one of the final four—because negative thoughts are useless—he went totally ballistic! I can still hear him barking at me, "A good soldier is always prepared for any eventuality, no matter how awful!"

I figured there was no sense in telling him I wasn't a soldier. Besides, I can't really be mad at him. He's just a dad who's trying to protect his little girl. I just wish I could make him see that I'm not a little girl anymore. I'm a senior in high school. I have to try things, and take a few risks.

Still, he did sign the permission forms that Eileen Kerr faxed to him. So, despite his own reservations, he IS backing me, in his own way. Now all I want to do is make him proud.

Wow! It's almost 12:00! I'd better get to sleep. Tomorrow is the most important day of my life. I want to be ready for it.

'Night.

Alyssa

Chapter 2

"Good morning, girls," Eileen Kerr greeted her eight new charges with a burst of energy that could only be described as a dynamite explosion. Eileen's booming, upbeat voice shocked Melanie into a more awake state than she'd ever experienced during the morning. Melanie was not a morning person. But, apparently, Eileen Kerr was. And that meant Melanie was going to have to reset her internal alarm clock if she wanted to get on Eileen's good side. The thought did not thrill her.

Although it was obvious to Melanie that Eileen was all business, the brownstone did not reflect her attitude. It was one thing to work for a totally efficient businessperson. But living in an office was a whole other thing. Luckily for Melanie and the others, the Omega brownstone was designed with teenage girls in mind. Sure, the bottom two floors housed studios, music rooms, and offices, but the rest of the brownstone was like a real home. The cafeteria looked more like a family dining room you'd find in a house, and the lounge area had a TV and a big, comfy couch—so it felt more like a family room than a study lounge. Not that Melanie was under any delusions that the girls she was sitting with right now would ever become family to her. She was just too different from any of them to ever feel that sort of attachment.

As Eileen began to speak, Melanie forced her personal thoughts from her head and paid close attention. She didn't want to miss anything important—and with someone like Eileen, everything was bound to be important!

"Well, today's the first day of training for No Secrets," Eileen began. "And let me warn you right now that we are gonna bust your buns for the next few months. By the time you leave this building, you will be prepared to be pop stars, whether or not you make the group," Eileen adjusted the plain brown headband that held her shoulder-length, sleek brown hair in place and smiled. "Now, let me introduce your coaches." She pointed to a tall, muscular man with a long blond ponytail. "This is Joseph. He's your trainer. In order to dance and sing at the same time, you're going to have to get into the best shape of your lives. And make no mistake, you will dance and sing at the same time. I do not tolerate lip-synching in my groups."

Eileen moved over and put her arm around Candace, the woman Melanie had met when she'd arrived the night before. "Candace is the best vocal coach in the country. She'll make sure you're on key all the time. She looks pretty sweet, but don't kid yourselves. I've seen Candace in action. If you're off by a note or a beat, she'll let you know. So I suggest rehearsing as much as you can."

Eileen leaned in front of Candace and turned her attention to a tall young woman with long brown hair that was pulled back in a ponytail. She was wearing an oversized sleeveless sweatshirt and running pants, but the baggy clothes did not hide her tight, muscular physique. "This is Sonia," Eileen introduced her. "Your dance coach. She'll be choreographing your dance numbers. Here's a hint: Keep your eyes and ears open at all times while you're working with her. Sonia's choreography can be more than tricky—and it has to be correctly performed by everyone, or the whole image of the group will appear sloppy."

Hannah could feel the nervous perspiration forming on her forehead already. This was the big league. Those coaches weren't going to be cutting anyone any slack. She used the sleeve of her white silk Prada blouse to wipe the sweat from her brow. The perspiration left little marks in the silk, but Hannah was too stressed to care.

"Now, maybe we should talk about the way things are going to run around here," Eileen told the girls. "We've split you into two groups of four, based mostly on where your voices fit in to the music. Those are the groups you'll be working with for the time being. It isn't like I'm going to pick all of group A or all of group B to be No Secrets, though. It's just that we need to work with you in smaller groups. Each girl will be judged on her own merits.

"Group A is made up of Alyssa, Daria, Serena, and Katie. Group B's members are Melanie, Janine, Cass, and Hannah. Your group schedules will be posted daily in the dining room."

Eileen took a short breath before continuing her opening lecture. "Each week your coaches and I will meet to discuss your progress. Then I'll speak to you all individually to let you know where we see your strengths and weaknesses to be. I'm telling you now, if you came here with any ego, you can check it at the door. In this brownstone, everyone is in the learning stage. You'll have to learn to take constructive criticism."

Janine glanced over at Daria. She of all people was going to have the toughest time checking her ego at the door. Janine knew it was a wicked thought, but she couldn't help but get excited at the thought of Daria having to sit and listen to other people's criticisms for a change.

"Your coaches and I are all here full time. If you want extra help, all you need to do is ask. We'll have a sign-up sheet with specific tutoring hours posted in the waiting room outside my office. And . . ."

Cass's head was spinning as she listened to Eileen drone on. There was so much to remember. Cass had heard that Eileen Kerr's training program was tough, but she'd never imagined this. When she'd worked on *The Kids Company*, everyone on the set had coddled her and treated her like a beloved pet. But this was very different. Eileen Kerr's program seemed really tough — even for someone who'd been out there in the real world. Cass couldn't even begin to imagine what the other girls might be thinking.

"Now, for the basic rules," Eileen continued. "No smoking, no drinking, and of course, no drugs. No boyfriends in the brownstone. Curfew is at ten o'clock every week night, twelve-thirty weekends. No exceptions! And don't think you'll be able to sneak in or out of here the way you may have done at PCBS. I've worked with musicians for the past twenty years — I know what they are capable of. No one will be able to get past me, I assure you."

Serena nudged Melanie in the side. She had a feeling that last bit had been added just for Mel's benefit. Melanie had to fight from rolling her eyes at her roommate's reminder of some of Melanie's past late-night adventures. She didn't want Eileen to think that she had any intention of breaking any of the Omega rules.

"The only night you will be allowed to stay out later than curfew is New Year's Eve," Eileen told the girls. "But even then, one o'clock is the curfew. I want you all back here and in your rooms by that time."

Katie shyly raised her hand. "That's only if we're staying at the brownstone over the holidays, right?"

Eileen looked at her curiously. "What are you talking about? You'll be here for New Year's Eve."

"But I thought we had the week between

Christmas and New Year's off," Katie continued.

Eileen shook her head. "PCBS has that schedule. But here, we have to keep working. I want to get No Secrets out on tour by the summer. That means no long breaks. You'll have Christmas Eve and Christmas Day to yourselves. But that's about it. I expect you all to be working the rest of the time."

Katie began to feel a nervous rumbling in her stomach. She wouldn't be going home for Christmas. How was she going to explain this one to Keith? They'd had such big plans for her winter vacation. He was never going to understand why she couldn't go to Texas for the week.

"Okay, that's about it," Eileen said finally. "Except that three hours a day you will all work with tutors on your schoolwork. You have to keep up your grades to stay in the Omega Talent training program. Again, no exceptions. Your schedules are already posted. Classes begin in fifteen minutes. Good luck to all of you."

As the girls filtered out into the hall, they were careful not to grumble or complain—at least until Eileen and her coaches were out of earshot.

"I'm telling you, the basic training my dad went through had nothing on this," Alyssa told Janine as they headed toward the dining room to check out their schedules. "This just may be worse than the army."

"I can't believe I won't be home for Christmas," Janine moaned. "I mean, it was bad enough spending Thanksgiving here. But, Christmas!" She paused and choked back a tear. "Hannah and Melanie are so lucky. They both live in New York. They'll get to go home for Christmas Eve at least."

"I don't think I'd want to spend Christmas with Hannah's or Melanie's families," Alyssa said simply.

Janine knew just what she meant. Melanie's family was pretty much the definition of "dysfunctional": Her mom had spent a lot of Melanie's childhood in drug rehab while Mel had stayed with her aunt. And Hannah's family—well, nobody knew a whole lot about the Lindens, except that they lived in some ritzy Park Avenue building. Despite the fact that Hannah lived right in the city, Janine knew it would never occur to her to invite the other girls to Christmas dinner.

"I guess missing Christmas is just the first of many sacrifices we'll have to make in order to do what we love for a living," Alyssa told her best pal. "At least we'll all be together."

Just then Daria sidled up alongside Janine. "Aren't you glad there's a workout coach?" she asked her. "I'll bet Eileen brought him in just for your benefit. You'll be able to fit in one seat on the subway in no time."

As Daria snickered and walked away, Janine pulled her blue sweatshirt down over her thighs. "So we'll all be together for Christmas," Janine mused as she watched Daria saunter off down the hall. "Is that a promise or a threat?"

Chapter 3

Katie sat down at her desk and pulled out her box of stationery. She stared at the blank sheet of paper for a long while. Then she scribbled down the words "Dear Keith."

Okay, at least she'd gotten started. But what was she supposed to write now? No matter what she put down on the paper, it wasn't going to soothe his hurt feelings. And it wasn't going to stop the inevitable angry phone call she'd get after he received her letter in the mail.

Quickly, Katie crumpled up the sheet of stationery and tossed it in the wastebasket below her desk. There was no way she was going to be able to write this the way she wanted to. And she didn't think she could handle sweating out the wait until Keith received her letter and called her back. And since Keith didn't believe in e-mails (he thought they were totally impersonal), that left only one option. Katie was going to have to call Keith, *today*.

She glanced over at her clock. It was 5:00 already.

That meant it was 4:00 in Houston. Keith would be home from school by now. Without giving herself a chance to change her mind, Katie picked up the phone and began to dial.

There were two rings. Katie was about to hang up and try again, when Keith's slow Texas drawl could be heard over the line. "Hello?"

"Keith!" Katie said, with far too much excitement in her voice. She made a mental note to calm down. She didn't want to let him know how anxious she really was. She wanted to take this conversation slow and easy, kind of let him down gently, and then hope he didn't get too angry.

"Sug?" Keith asked. "What's wrong? I thought you weren't going to call me till Wednesday. Did something happen up there?"

"No, not really," Katie replied nervously. "I just wanted to hear your voice."

"'Not really'?" Keith asked, immediately picking up on the stress in Katie's voice. "What's that supposed to mean?"

"Well, it's not a big thing, actually, it's just that, well—"

"What?" Keith demanded. "Stop stalling and just tell me."

"Okay. It's just that we got our schedules, and I won't be able to get home for Christmas after all," Katie began. "But I was thinking you might want to come here, since I have my evenings free, and we could spend New Year's Eve together and—"

"What do you mean I should come to you?" Keith's reaction was more volatile than Katie had expected. "I'm not coming to New York City for Christmas. Christmas is a family holiday. You're supposed to spend it at home—with the people you love!"

"Well, we could spend the day with each other. We could pretend that your hotel room is our home. Put a tree in there or something."

"I'd have to stay in a hotel?" Keith asked her.

"Well, there're no boys allowed here," Katie said. "But since Christmas Eve is a Friday night, I don't have to be back until twelve-thirty. That leaves plenty of time to—"

"You mean you'd come to my hotel room, but you wouldn't want to be there for breakfast in bed the next morning? You'd just get dressed and go home in the middle of the night?"

Katie blushed the way she always did when Keith alluded to their sex life. "It's the rule, Keith. We have curfews. Anyhow, it's not so different from the way things were back home. I never stayed over at your house, either. You know our folks would've killed us if they'd found us . . . that way."

"Yeah, well, I don't like the idea that you're so willing to go to a man's hotel room to fool around. You'd never even have considered that before you went to New York. What's gotten into you, Katherine?"

Katherine. He'd used her given name. Keith was obviously really mad now. Her head was spinning

24

wildly. Keith was turning all her words around. He was trying to pick a fight. "Not just any man's room, Keith. Your room. Our room. I love you, Keith. I want to spend Christmas with you."

"Well, I wanted to spend the rest of my life with you, Katie. But I'm not going be the kind of man who chases his girl around the globe. Your place is here with me, and you know it. Stop playing this game and come home where you belong. You know how good things felt when you were here with me this past weekend. That's the way it could be—should be—for us."

There was something dark and foreboding in Keith's voice that hadn't ever been there before. Katie could feel the anger through the phone lines. She wanted to hang up before the argument got even more out of hand.

But she was too late.

"Katie, you've gotta make a choice," Keith insisted. "Right now. Either you come home for Christmas break, or I can't guarantee that this relationship will ever be the same again."

"But Keith, I can't come home. Eileen Kerr made it very clear that we're back at work on the twenty-sixth, no exceptions. If I blow that, I'm out of the band before I even make it. And I want this so badly, Keith."

For a moment, there was silence on the other end. "Then I guess you've made your decision. Happy holidays, Katie. And don't worry about me. I'm sure I won't be lonely without you."

And with that, Keith hung up the phone.

Katie just sat there on her bed, stunned. She wasn't even sure if what had just happened wasn't some sort of dream. No, not a dream. A nightmare! But as she stared at the phone that was cradled in her hand, she knew that Keith really had said all those horrible, cruel things.

The tears started coming then. She couldn't seem to stop them, even as she heard Daria entering the room. She hadn't wanted to cry in front of her.

"Oh God, what now?" Daria moaned in her clipped Chicago accent. "Keith again?"

Katie nodded slowly.

"Ugh," Daria exclaimed. "I feel like I'm living in the middle of a soap opera. And I am so ready to change the channel."

Katie stood up and threw the phone across the room in a moment of uncharacteristic anger. Daria ducked out of its path just in time.

"Screw you, Daria!" Katie shouted, her Texas drawl suddenly sounding anything but demure. Then she turned and raced out of the room.

"Sheesh," Daria sputtered, as she placed the phone back into its base. "Some people are soooo touchy."

Cass was just coming up the stairs as Katie raced out of her room. Katie was so upset, she almost ran right into her.

"Whoa!" Cass exclaimed. "Slow down." She looked at Katie's tear-stained face. "What's wrong?"

Katie didn't—couldn't—answer her.

Cass put her arm around Katie. "Look, let's go in my room, okay? The last thing you want is for Eileen or one of her staff to see you like this on your very first day."

Katie nodded gratefully and let Cass steer her into her dorm room. She was more than glad to allow someone take care of her for a moment.

Janine was sitting at her desk puzzling over an economics formula in her textbook when the girls entered the room. She quickly closed the book when she saw the state that Katie was in. "What happened?" she asked.

Cass shrugged. "She won't say. But my guess is it's Keith again." She looked at Katie. "Is that it?"

Katie nodded slowly.

Janine sat down on the bed next to Katie. "You told him about Christmas, huh?"

Again Katie nodded.

"I guess he didn't take it too well," Cass said gently.

"He basically told me he was going to spend the holiday with someone else!" The words nearly exploded from Katie's lips.

"Oh God, it's happening again." Cassidy sighed.

Janine looked at her curiously. "What do you mean, again? Keith's given her grief before, but he never threatened to start seeing someone else."

Cass shook her head. "No, I know. It's just that this seems to happen all the time whenever I'm in a work situation. One person in a relationship has a chance at fame, and the other person can't handle that. Keith's just jealous of all the excitement in your life."

"I think Cass is right. Maybe he'll come around when he sees how happy you are," Janine suggested.

Katie looked down at the floor and tried to catch her breath. "I don't think so. And I'm not so sure I want him to."

Janine and Cass seemed surprised. They weren't quite certain how to react to that. Katie was so in love with Keith. Why wouldn't she want him back?

"Keith says I've changed since I moved to New York. I think he's right. He was talking about spending our whole lives together—y'know, having a home in Texas, and all that. But I'm not ready to plan my whole life right now. I want to see things, experience new adventures. I can't settle down while I'm still a teenager. And I can't be what he needs."

Cass smiled. "Good for you!" she cheered her friend. "You get it. You really get what it's all about. It's almost impossible to keep up a relationship when you're in a pop band. You're always on the road. There's never any time to work on a relationship—and the kind of commitment Keith is talking about does take a lot of time. You are definitely too young to close off your options right now. You'll only resent him for it in the end."

Katie listened to Cass. She knew she was speaking from experience. Cass didn't say much about her home life, but she had mentioned that her mother had once been a struggling actress—before she'd met and married Cass's dad at eighteen. Cass was just a little kid when her mom realized that she missed "the biz." That's when Cass's folks had split up. Her dad moved to San Francisco, and Cass's mom dedicated her life to turning her daughter into the star she herself had never become.

"Look, if Keith is going to see other people, there's no reason you can't do the same. There are plenty of other fish in the sea," Cass assured her. "You've only dated one guy in your whole life. You need to get out more—find out what other options you might have. I think you may be surprised at the many different kinds of men there are out there."

Janine grinned at Katie. "Yeah, and if you decide you don't like any of those fish out there, will you throw one my way? I haven't had a date in ages."

Katie forced herself to smile at Janine. "I don't know if I can do that right now, y'all. It's not my style. I think I'll steer clear of guys for a while. I need to focus on No Secrets right now."

"Not tonight, you don't," Cass disagreed. "Tonight you just have to focus on which flavor of Ben & Jerry's you want to dive into. That's what you do when you have man troubles. You pig out on ice cream!"

Katie studied Cass's stick-thin physique. "You want to have ice cream?" she asked, barely hiding the skepticism in her voice.

"Sure!" Cass told her. "But I'm warning you—I get first dibs on the Cherry Garcia!"

Self-Expression Journal

Today was exhausting! And I don't just mean because of the intense workout Joseph put us through in the gym this afternoon. I mean emotionally. I'm so worried about my friends that I haven't had time to be nervous or anxious about spending the next few months in this brownstone. All I can think about is how Katie is taking her breakup with Keith, and what I can do to help Cass with this eating issue she's got going.

For the longest time I've been so jealous of Cass's figure. I know jealousy is a wasted emotion (or so Alyssa reminds me constantly!), but it's impossible for me not to want to look like Cass. She's so thin, clothes always seem to look like they were made for her. I'll bet she's never had to wonder what her bathing suit looks like from behind.

But today I was finally faced with the reality of how Cass stays that way. I guess I always knew deep down that she had a problem; I just didn't want to believe it. But after what happened tonight, I have to.

Cass, Katie, and I really pigged out on ice cream. Well, Katie and Cass did. I only had a little bit—I've gotta watch it. Still, I was kinda surprised to see Cass chomping on a whole pint of Cherry Garcia.

Then, when I went into the bathroom to brush my teeth, I heard someone throwing up in the bathroom. So I asked whoever it was if she was okay. It turned out to be Cass. She made some lame excuse about being lactose intolerant and how the ice cream made her nauseated, but I know that's not the truth.

The question is, how do I deal with this? If I tell her mom, she'll just tell me to mind my own business—Alana's so hooked on having a daughter that looks as perfect as Cass that she wouldn't care how Cass managed to keep up her looks. And I can't tell Eileen or any of the coaches, because that would destroy Cass's chance at making the band. I can't even tell the other girls, for fear it might get out.

I know I should just confront Cass, but somehow I know she'll deny it, or lie like she did tonight. I don't know what to do. I guess I'll just have to hope that Cass will shake this eating problem on her own.

Although somehow I don't have high hopes for that.

Janine

Chapter 4

Cass hopped out of the shower, slipped on her robe, wrapped a towel around her wet head, and headed back to her room. It was Saturday morning—the first day she didn't have to make an early morning class or workout. She felt relaxed—or as relaxed as anyone could feel in the competitive atmosphere of the brownstone.

But as she entered her room, Cass felt the familiar nervous fluttering in her stomach. The red light was blinking on her answering machine. That light always stressed Cass out. There was always a chance that the call could be from her mother.

But when Cass looked at her clock, she realized that it was only ten o'clock in the morning—seven o'clock in Los Angeles. Since her mother was definitely *not* an early riser, the call couldn't possibly have been from her. Cass felt her whole body relax with the realization.

Cass pushed the play button and waited for the machine to rewind. Then she sat back and listened.

"Cassidy, honey," the message began. Cass begin to feel her pulse quicken. It was her mom after all. Why was she calling so early?

"Surprise! I'm here in New York," Cass's mother's message continued. "I'm staying at the Parker Meridien—the Plaza was all filled up. I've been invited to a Christmas Eve party and I thought I'd come a few weeks early just to help you get settled into your new routine. I'll be here until New Year's, so we can spend lots of time together.

"I'm free for dinner tonight—so I'll pick you up about seven thirty. I can't wait to see your room! Do you think Eileen Kerr will be there? I'd love to speak with her. I think we met at a party in the Hollywood Hills last year, and I'm sure we have mutual friends . . ."

Cass could barely hear the words as her mother cheerfully chatted on into the machine. All Cass could think about was that her mother was coming to the brownstone—tonight! As usual, Alana Morgan hadn't considered the idea that her daughter might have plans of her own—it wouldn't have mattered, anyway, since Alana expected Cass to drop everything when she came to town. And Cass always did just that.

As the message came to a close, Cass leaped up and started rummaging wildly through her closet, looking for an outfit her mother would approve of. By the time Janine walked into the room the two girls shared, the entire floor was filled with castoffs that Cass thought were too inappropriate for dinner with her ever-critical mother.

"What're you doing?" Janine asked as she stepped over a pair of black suede Kenneth Cole pumps and scooted to the left to avoid tripping over a silver Kate Spade pocketbook.

"Looking for an outfit for tonight."

Janine sat on her bed and folded her knees under her chin. "Oooh! Got a big date?"

Cass shook her head. "I should be so lucky. No, my mom's in town. She called to take me out to dinner. And that means I have to find a dress that won't show all that ice cream we chowed down the other night."

Janine frowned but didn't say anything as she watched the stick-thin Cass hold skirt after skirt over her narrow hips. She knew Cass hadn't absorbed any of those calories, and she was confused as to why Cass would think she had.

"You'll look great in anything," Janine assured her. "Besides, she's your mom. She'll just be glad to see you."

Cass shot Janine a grateful smile. She knew her roommate was doing her best to be supportive. But neither one of them believed that the overly ambitious Alana Morgan would ever be completely satisfied with Cass.

"How long's your mom in town for?" Janine asked.

"Till New Year's." Cass sighed.

"Oh, good! Then you two can spend Christmas together. You're so lucky!"

But Cass didn't look happy at the prospect of

exchanging gifts with her mother. "I was kinda looking forward to spending the holiday with you guys," Cass told her. "Believe me, it would be a lot less pressure than trying to buy the perfect gift for Mom. Not that it matters what I buy her—she always returns my gifts no matter what they are."

"Speaking of gifts," Janine began, trying to lighten the conversation, "where are we ever going to find gifts that cost less than ten dollars in this city?"

"I don't know," Cass admitted as she slid an oversized purple mohair sweater over her head. "Alyssa was really adamant about insisting that we all get everyone a gift. I mean, why not do a Secret Santa again this year? It's so much easier to buy a couple of small gifts for one person than it is to buy one gift for each girl."

"I think Alyssa felt sorry for whoever might wind up with Daria as their Secret Santa. Remember last year when she gave Serena all those packs of breath mints wrapped in a bow, with a note that they were for her next date? She knows Serena has never even been out on a date in her whole life. It was really mean of her to rub it in like that. And to make it worse, for the rest of the year, Serena was convinced she had bad breath. She was constantly gargling with mouthwash!"

"Maybe the real Santa will leave Daria a lump of coal this year," Cass suggested.

"If he doesn't, I just might," Janine replied. "That is, if I ever have time to buy any Christmas presents."

"I thought you were going shopping with Katie today."

"I was," Janine admitted. "But I had to cancel. First, I have to finish my analysis of *The Children's Hour* for theater lit. class. And then I want to work on that new song Candace threw at us. We have to have all the lyrics memorized by Monday afternoon. Katie's going on her own."

"Do you think she's going to buy a gift for Keith?" Cass asked.

"I don't know. I don't think he's sent her a letter or called or anything since they had that big blowout. And it's been five days since then," Janine told her. "I just wish she'd dump him and move on."

Katie sat on her bed and reread the letter in her hand for a third time. She could hardly believe what she'd seen. But there were the words, written in her friend Lyndsey's round, large hand.

"I thought you'd be better off hearing this from a friend, Katie," the letter read. "Keith's been spending a whole lot of time with Sue-Ann Sims these days. And there's been some gossip about those two. Something about Keith and Sue-Ann ditchin' school and making out behind his daddy's toolshed. I mean, it's just rumors, Katie, but with that girl's reputation, the stories could be true. And I thought somebody should tell you."

Katie knew all about Sue-Ann's reputation. She'd earned that rep, one boy at a time. If people thought

Sue-Ann and Keith were making out, it was probably true. In fact, it was more than likely they'd gone further than that.

But Katie also knew what Keith thought about girls like Sue-Ann. He felt that girls who put out for everyone in town were cheap, and not worth a second look. For a while, Katie felt guilty. Keith had to be pretty lonely to turn to Sue-Ann for comfort. And that was Katie's fault.

But before long, the guilt was replaced with anger. Katie was plenty lonely, too. And she was in just as much pain as Keith was. She may've been in New York living out part of her dream, but she was missing a lot, too—like the fact that she would surely have been the junior class homecoming queen this year. And then there was the Christmas ball, and going caroling with her cousins on Christmas Eve. Those were all things Katie would have loved to have been doing right about now.

She and Keith were both disappointed about how this Christmas was turning out. The difference was Keith was with Sue-Ann, and Katie wasn't with anyone. She wasn't just making out with any guy she could find just because she was missing Keith. She'd been faithful to him—for years now.

Suddenly, Katie had to get out of the brownstone—and away from Lyndsey's letter. She threw on her jacket, grabbed her pocketbook, and raced out of the building. A Saturday afternoon of Christmas shopping was just what she needed.

Chapter 5

Katie strapped her pocketbook over her chest as she browsed through the men's department in Bloomingdale's. If there was one thing she was aware of during the Christmas season, it was pickpockets. The city had created an all-out advertising campaign warning people that their wallets could be stolen at any moment, since the stores were all so crowded with people hunting for holiday bargains. Katie wasn't in the mood to have her allowance money stolen from her on top of everything else.

So when a tall, good-looking guy with straight, chestnut-brown hair bumped into Katie by the sweater table, her first reaction was to grab her bag for dear life. The boy studied her swift, defensive action and laughed. "Sorry," he apologized. "And don't worry—I didn't take your wallet."

Katie blushed a beet red. "I, uh, I didn't think you'd taken my . . ."

A wide smile appeared on the guy's face, forcing his piercing brown eyes to crinkle up. "Yes, you did.

And that's okay. I could've been trying to take your money. But I wasn't. I was just trying to find a way to meet you."

Katie looked surprised and more than slightly nervous. "You were?"

"You bet. I've been watching you shop for the past twenty minutes. And since I couldn't come up with a great opening line, I figured I'd just bump into you and hope you'd be swept up by my obvious charisma." He smiled again, just to show that he was only teasing. Then he held out his hand. "I'm Jackson Warner."

Katie laughed and shook his hand. "Katie Marr."

"Okay, so now we're no longer total strangers," he said with a twinkle in his eye. "Which is a good thing, because I'll bet your mother told you to never talk to strangers."

"Yes, she did," Katie agreed, laughing.

"But since we're not strangers anymore, how'd you like to have lunch and get better acquainted? I'm starving, and I think I noticed a sushi bar on the next block."

Katie wrinkled up her nose and shook her head. Raw fish was not her idea of food.

"Okay, no sushi," Jackson assured her. "How 'bout we go to that diner down the block? They've got everything."

Katie's immediate reaction was to thank Jackson for the offer and then tell him she was sorry, but she had a boyfriend. But the truth was, Katie wasn't so sure she had a boyfriend anymore. And it was only a meal, after all. It wasn't like she was making out with this handsome guy behind a toolshed or anything! "You're on," Katie told him. "I'm getting pretty tired of shopping, anyhow."

"Good," Jackson replied. "Then we'll have the whole afternoon to get to know each other better."

While Katie had been busy shopping in Bloomingdale's, Hannah was walking through FairBuy, a produce store on Broadway, looking for some healthy snacks to keep in her dorm room. Hannah had learned all about FairBuy from her mother. Mrs. Linden often shopped for her boss's groceries there. It was way across town from their Park Avenue apartment, but the Aldens wouldn't settle for anything less than the freshest foods.

Now that Hannah had moved uptown, her biggest nightmare was that she might be with the other girls when she bumped into her mother. She knew just how her mom would look, in her old wool coat, dragging a cart of food as she purchased the ingredients to make dinner for the Aldens.

Not that Hannah was ashamed of her mother. She really wasn't. Hannah knew that her mom worked hard and earned an honest living. It was just that Hannah's mother had no idea that her daughter had led her classmates to believe that her family was wealthy enough to have an apartment on Park Avenue. And Hannah's housemates had no clue that she and her mother lived in the small, cramped servants' quarters of the Aldens' apartment. Hannah was simply afraid that her mother would blow her cover.

So, in an effort to keep her secret intact, Hannah usually made up some excuse not to tag along when her housemates shopped at the places her mother frequented. The other girls might've figured she was a snob, but it just seemed safer that way. Of course, the result of all her secrecy was that Hannah was alone a lot of the time.

As Hannah walked out of FairBuy, her fruits and vegetables in hand, she spotted Melanie across the street. Melanie was loaded down with music paper and her portable keyboard. Hannah figured that she was on her way home from playing Christmas Carols on the street and passing the hat. It was a cash-earning gig that Eileen Kerr would probably disapprove of, but had never actually banned it.

Despite the fact that Mel was usually downright cruel to Hannah—calling her "Princess" and goading her about the privileged life she assumed Hannah led—she still had to give the girl credit: Melanie had refused to change who she was to fit some image Eileen Kerr might've wanted her to convey. She had stayed completely true to herself—a trait Hannah herself had never managed to develop.

Just then a gray Mercedes pulled over to the curb beside Hannah. A woman in a thick, dark, mink coat peeked her head out from the rear window. "Hannah, is that you?" the woman asked in an upper-crust

Connecticut accent. "Come, let me give you a lift."

Hannah turned her attention away from Melanie and smiled as sweetly as she could to the woman in the car. "Thank you, Mrs. Alden," she replied as she reached to open the rear door of the car.

Mrs. Alden shook her head. "You know what, dear, I have a million packages in the back with me. Why don't you ride up front with James? He'll take you wherever you need to go after he helps me with these bags."

Hannah nodded and opened the front door of the car. She understood exactly what Mrs. Alden meant. In every car there was a backseat and a front seat. Hannah's place was beside the driver, in front of the clear-glass partition, where the servants sat.

As they pulled away, Hannah could only hope that Melanie hadn't seen her get into the Mercedes. She could only imagine what Mel would've thought about that.

I can't believe what Hannah did to me today. I know she saw me standing there on Broadway, lugging my keyboard and my music. Would it have been so hard for her to just offer me a ride? She didn't try to explain, or even say she was sorry, when she saw me walk past her dorm room. She just turned away and acted as though she didn't see me . . . again.

Man, that girl is gonna have to change her attitude if she's gonna be part of this band. I don't get the feeling Eileen Kerr is big on people having special privileges. Hannah won't be flying first class when the rest of us are in coach, if you know what I mean.

Maybe Hannah oughtta pray she doesn't make the band. Then she can go back to her pleasant little debutante life and marry some guy her rich daddy will choose for her. She can be just like her mom, shopping all day and going to her little charity events at night.

I hate that girl sometimes! I was freezing by the time I got home. And then I had to go back to my room and face Serena. She'd just put up another one of her cutesy posters. This one's one of those hideous retro smiley-face posters — you know, the kind that say, "Have a Happy Day"? It was all I could do to keep myself from drawing a mustache on its ugly yellow head!

But I have to shake all this negative energy. It isn't going to get me anywhere. I feel a little less angry just spilling my guts into this journal. But I think I'll feel even better if I go beat up a punching bag in the basement gym for a while. I can picture Hannah's face on one side of the bag, and Serena's smiley-face poster on the other. That oughtta do it!

Melanie

Chapter 6

The phone rang early in Katie and Daria's room. Daria rolled over and moaned out loud. "Will you get that? It's probably one of your annoying friends calling to fill you in on your ex-boyfriend's latest sexcapade."

Katie rubbed her eyes, sat up, and picked up the receiver. "Hello?" she said, barely masking the sleep in her voice.

"Well, hello to you, too," a familiar-sounding male voice replied.

Suddenly Katie was wide awake. A grin spread across her lips. He'd actually called her! What a wonderful way to start the day! Katie glanced over at Daria's grumpy expression. "Hold on while I take the phone in the hall with me," she whispered into the receiver.

"Jackson," Katie exclaimed once she'd settled herself on the floor in the hallway. "What are you doing up so early?"

"Happy anniversary," he congratulated Katie.

"What?"

Jackson sighed dramatically. "Oh, no. Don't tell me you've forgotten already. It's exactly eighteen hours since we met."

Katie giggled. "Oh, well. Forgive me. Happy anniversary, then."

"Thank you," Jackson replied as he and Katie shared a small laugh.

Instinctively, Katie knew that this would always be their private joke. It seemed strange that she would be sharing something intimate like that with a guy she had met only a day before. But then again, she'd felt comfortable with Jackson from the very start.

"What kind of anniversary is this?" she asked. "I know the one-year anniversary is paper, and twenty-five years is silver. But I don't think anyone has named the eighteen-hour anniversary yet."

"Then let's call it the scrambled eggs anniversary. Meet me for breakfast at the diner we went to yesterday."

"I can't go all the way to Midtown," Katie told him. "I have to be at a recording studio seminar in two hours."

"So miss it," Jackson said. "I have much more exciting plans in store for us."

I'll bet you do, Katie thought excitedly to herself. "It's tempting," she admitted. "But we have our first critiques in about a week, and I don't want to mess anything up with Eileen right now."

"Okay, then, I'll meet you uptown," Jackson suggested, sounding only mildly disappointed. "How 'bout at that little coffee shop on Eighty-third and Columbus?"

Katie smiled. The boy was definitely persistent. "Okay, I'll meet you there in half an hour," she agreed.

As Katie returned to the room, Daria opened her eyes and studied her roommate's glowing face. "What're you so happy about?" she snarled from under her covers. "Did your lover boy call and make things all better?"

Katie knew Daria had to be talking about Keith. Just the mention of him made her feel guilty—like she was cheating or something. But that didn't make any sense. After all, Katie wasn't cheating on Keith. She was simply having breakfast with a friend.

Of course she'd never changed her clothes four times to meet any of her other friends at a coffee shop.

I think I'm homesick. Genuinely homesick. I haven't felt this way the whole time I've been in New York. But tonight I just wish I were tucked in, safe in my own little bed in Iowa.

I know Melanie thinks it's weird that I've been sleeping with my old fuzzy bunny tonight—— I mean, what sixteen-year-old actually sleeps with a stuffed toy? But I don't care what she thinks. Right now I need to hold on to something. And Mr. Bunny is all I've got.

It's just that I'm so nervous! We've got our very first critique coming up in just one week, and I'm not sure what Eileen and our coaches think about me. I know I had trouble following that dance routine Sonia had us try yesterday, and that's sure to count against me. And I don't think I sing as well as some of the other girls in my group. I'm working on improving my range, but sometimes I think all those vocal exercises are a total waste of time. There're a whole list of problems I'm having—— and I don't think any of them have slipped by Eileen.

I keep telling myself that this is all constructive criticism. And that everyone is going to have something that they have to work on. I just hope I don't burst into tears at the first issue Eileen points out to me. That would be so embarrassing, and unprofessional.

At least I won't have to go first. Eileen posted the schedule today, and Alyssa's critique is the earliest one. But in some ways, she's lucky. She'll get it over with first thing in the morning. I have to wait until after lunch.

　　Oh, this week is going to last forever!

Serena

Chapter 7

Cass was sitting in the waiting room outside Eileen Kerr's office when Alyssa emerged from her critique. Cass didn't like the expression on Alyssa's face as she inched closer toward the couch where Cass was sitting. Her eyes seemed glazed over, and there was a gray, ashen look to her skin.

"That bad, huh?" Cass asked with a mixture of kindness and nervousness in her voice.

"Let's just say Eileen Kerr shoots straight. She doesn't sugarcoat any of the bad stuff."

Now Cass could feel herself getting nervous. Alyssa had one of the best voices in the brownstone. And her dancing was really great, too. If Eileen and the coaches had torn Alyssa apart, what would they do to her?

"Look, it's not that bad," Alyssa assured her. "Just a lot more intense than anything we experienced at PCBS. Eileen says that's because there's a lot more at stake here."

Alyssa looked at Cass's nervous, wrinkled brow.

Suddenly she felt the need to protect her fragile, high-strung friend from any unnecessary stress. "Hey, at least it's better than the army. Eileen didn't make me clean the whole latrine with a toothbrush just because I'm sometimes off by a beat in my dancing," she teased.

Cass forced a smile to her face. She knew Alyssa was trying to calm her down. Unfortunately, it wasn't working.

Alyssa returned Cass's smile with a weak grin. "Just one helpful hint, though. She's gonna start out with all the good stuff. But don't be fooled. As soon as you're feeling good about yourself, she'll come in for the kill."

"Gee thanks," Cass replied sarcastically. "I feel so much better now."

Alyssa shrugged. "I'm just warning you, that's all. Besides, you've been through this stuff before. Maybe it won't seem so bad to you."

Cass frowned. Actually, she'd never been through anything like this before. On the set of *The Kids Company*, the adult cast and crew members probably would've killed anyone who had made Cass feel bad about herself. They were all her protectors. For a long time, Cass didn't understand why the grown-ups all seemed devoted to her personally—after all, there were plenty of other kids on the set. But one day she overheard two grips talking. "Somebody should arrest that mother for child abuse," one of them had said. "She's got that poor little girl working all week, and then on the weekends she piles on the personal engagements. The kid never rests. My wife keeps saying she wants to adopt her and show her what it's really like to be a kid. You know Cass has never had a playdate, or just gone swimming—without doing a photo shoot first."

"I know," the second grip had responded. "I feel really bad for little Cassidy. But at least she has us."

That was the first time Cass had realized that not all child actors spent as much time in an adult world as she did. But Cass didn't see her mother's efforts on her behalf as abuse. She saw it as love. Her mother was simply doing what was best for Cass. Alana was working hard to see that Cass had a future in show business. And Cass believed she had to do her part, too, so that their dreams could come true.

"Cass, come on in," Candace's sweet voice shook Cass from her thoughts.

Cass stood up and walked into Eileen's office. Eileen was sitting behind her desk. Candace, Joseph, and Sonia were in chairs beside her. The only place left for Cass to sit was on the couch across from them.

Eileen glanced at her notes. "Well, Cass, I don't have to tell you how pleased we are that you've brought your knowledge of professional performing to the brownstone. The other girls can certainly look to you as a leader. And that's an important position to hold."

Cass smiled, but remembered to keep herself from getting too relaxed. Alyssa had warned her that Eileen would start off easy.

"Your voice is magnificent. You have a wonderful range, and Candace says that you pick up harmonies very quickly."

"Thank you," Cass replied, looking gratefully at Candace.

"Oh, don't thank us," Eileen told her. "The things we say in here aren't compliments or criticisms. I simply state the facts as they are."

"Yes, ma'am," Cass said quietly.

"Okay, then. Sonia feels that your ability to memorize choreography is pretty good," Eileen continued. "But the problem is, you don't seem to have a lot of energy when you dance. You do the steps, but there's no *oomph*, if you know what I mean. And we need energy onstage, if the audience is going to feel the positive vibes we want them to."

"You seem to be dragging lately," Sonia interjected. "Just going through the motions."

"I noticed that in your workouts, too, Cass. You break into a sweat after the lightest weight training. You need to pick up your stamina. And your muscle tone needs to be worked on as well."

Cass wasn't sure how to respond—or even if she was supposed to. She *had* been a little tired lately. But she didn't think it was that big of a deal. Apparently, Eileen disagreed.

"The thing is, you're used to taped performances," Eileen explained. "If things aren't going right, you can take a break, have a drink of OJ, and bring the energy level up for the next take. But there are no second takes when you're performing live, Cass. So you have to be in top condition—all the time. Joseph's gonna put you on a nutrition plan, and an aerobic, weight-lifting program that should build your stamina. You need to follow it, okay?"

Cass nodded, but didn't say a word.

"Okay that's it," Eileen finished with a smile. "Send in the next victim on your way out."

That night, there was a lot less of the usual cheerful chatter in the brownstone dining room. Everyone seemed a little shell-shocked by Eileen's comments about their performances. No one argued that the criticisms were unfair; it was just that the girls were taking each of Eileen's comments to heart. After all, only four of the girls were going to wind up in No Secrets. And any one of a girl's professional failings could be the reason she would be one of the four asked to leave.

"I thought I was reaching those high notes pretty well," Janine moaned as she munched on her Caesar salad. "Certainly better than I ever had before. But now I have about fifty vocal exercises a night to do, to strengthen my voice. This is so depressing."

Hannah sighed. "I wonder why Eileen bothered to choose me at all. "

Serena nodded her head in agreement. "I know what you mean. Eileen told me I need more 'attitude' when I dance. I mean, how are you supposed to develop 'attitude', anyway? Isn't it something you're born with?"

"Hey, why're you looking at me?" Melanie interjected.

"I . . . um . . . ," Serena stammered. She hadn't realized she was looking in Melanie's direction.

"Maybe because you have attitude to spare," Alyssa gently chided her.

"I do, at least according to Eileen," Melanie allowed.

Daria listened carefully as her housemates discussed their critiques. She made mental notes of all the comments they had received. But she was careful not to reveal any of what had gone on during her meeting with Eileen. There was no sense in letting the others know what her weaknesses were.

For once, it seemed as though the other girls felt the same way Daria did. Although they were a bit more forthcoming with information than she was, they were definitely holding back plenty of the details from one another. Nobody seemed to want to give up too many particulars of her meeting with Eileen. For the very first time, the girls in the Omega brownstone saw each other as competitors—each vying for Eileen Kerr's approval. None of the girls wanted to admit that Eileen had been tougher on her than she'd been on the others.

"Has anybody seen Katie?" Serena asked. "I wonder how her critique went."

"I saw her for a few minutes after my meeting with Eileen. Her critique must not have been too awful, because she had a huge grin on her face," Janine replied. "It was good to see her smiling. In fact, the past few days she's seemed happier than she has been in a long time. Anyway, she said she was running late and had to leave. She hasn't been back here since."

"Maybe her critique was so awful, she decided to just hop on the first plane back to the Lone Star State," Daria replied.

"If that were the case, she wouldn't have been smiling," Janine countered.

"I don't know about that," Daria replied. "If Katie went back to Texas, I'd sure be smiling!"

"Hey, Janine, how'd Cass's critique go?" Alyssa asked, trying to stop Janine from getting into an argument with Daria. "She seemed pretty nervous when I saw her this morning."

Janine shrugged. "I don't know. The minute she got back to the room her mother called—I swear that woman has ESP or something. Anyway, she and Cass made plans to meet for dinner, and that's the last I saw of her."

"Okay, so what'd Eileen have to say?" Alana Morgan asked her daughter as the two ate dinner at a quiet little French restaurant in the East Thirties. Cass was relieved that for once her mother hadn't chosen one of the New York hot spots for their dinner conversation. Of course Cass understood the reason behind Alana's dinner choice: Alana didn't want any of the entertainment crowd in the city to overhear their conversation. Cass's mother felt that criticism was dirty laundry—and it should be kept well-hidden.

Cass pushed her salad Niçoise around on her plate and chose her words carefully. "Well, she loves my voice," she began slowly.

"Naturally," Alana replied with a smile. "All those singing lessons I arranged for have really paid off. What about your dancing, though?"

Cass sighed. That was her mother. Even when she was a little girl, Alana never seemed satisfied. Cass could remember proudly showing her mother a math test in which she'd scored a 98 percent. But instead of congratulating her daughter, Alana had demanded to know why Cass had fouled up on two of the questions!

"My dancing's pretty good," Cass assured her mother. "They're happy with the way I follow choreography."

"But . . . ," Alana probed.

"But," Cass continued, "they say I need to display a bit more energy when I perform."

Alana's face fell. "Oh, for goodness' sake, Cassie. Why would you choose this time in your career to slow down? This is no time for relaxing."

"I'm not relaxing, Mother. I was just focusing so hard on learning the routines that I took things a little slower. But they're second nature now, so I'll be able to give the routines all I've got."

"Well, I should hope so," Alana replied. "Haven't I always told you to smile and act like you're enjoying yourself?"

Cass frowned. Most mothers would tell their daughters to actually enjoy themselves. But not Alana. For her it was all about appearances. "Yes, Mother," Cass replied finally.

"Anything else?" Alana asked, without any attempt to hide the disappointment in her voice.

"Just that they're going to put me on some sort of nutrition plan, starting tomorrow."

Alana smiled at that. "Well, good. I didn't like the idea of your rooming with that Janine, Cass. She obviously doesn't watch what she eats. I was afraid you were going to pick up her bad habits. But I feel better knowing that Eileen is going to make sure you stay in shape. Remember, darling, as they say in *Cosmo*, 'You can never be too rich or too thin!'"

Cass didn't reply. She knew that Eileen wasn't afraid of Cass becoming heavy—not that Janine was actually heavy or anything. In fact, deep down, Cass suspected that Eileen was worried that she had become too thin. And that made Cass concerned that there was going to be far too much food on the nutrition plan. But of course Cass didn't reveal her feelings to Alana. She felt as though she'd already told her mother way too much.

"Okay, now that that's settled, let's move on to Christmas. Guess what—I got you an invitation to the Christmas Eve party at the Savins'. Their celebrating at their New York duplex instead of their Bel Air mansion. Something about wanting a *real* Christmas this year. Can you imagine? What's so unreal about Christmas in LA?"

Cass laughed despite herself. What was her mother talking about? As far as Cass was concerned, there was nothing real about LA, at Christmas or any other time of the year.

"I thought maybe you could get a white gown and I could get a similar one in black. That way, when we make our entrance . . ."

Cass listened halfheartedly as her mother droned on about the Christmas plans she'd made for them—without consulting Cass, of course. Somehow this wasn't the holiday Cass had hoped for. But then Cass's hopes weren't always her mother's top priority.

Katie stared at the hotel room clock in disbelief. Eleven forty-five! Oh, no! She must've fallen asleep. Now she had only forty-five minutes to get back to the brownstone before the weekend curfew.

As Katie struggled to button her blouse, a wave of guilt flooded over her. She couldn't believe she was here, alone in a hotel room, with a guy she'd only met a few days ago. This was everything Keith had warned her would take place if she stayed in New York. How had this happened to her? Why had she let him seduce her?

But as she looked over at Jackson's peacefully sleeping body, Katie realized that she hadn't been seduced at all. In fact, this had been every bit as much her idea as it had been his. Ever since she'd met Jackson she'd been flirting mercilessly with him, meeting him for clandestine breakfasts, and amorous walks in the snow. They'd even taken the Staten Island ferry together one afternoon. What could be more romantic than huddling together to stay warm against the winter winds? So when Jackson had kissed her, she'd just let it happen.

Still, Katie wasn't sure if she'd slept with Jackson because she liked him, or to get back at Keith, or just to prove to herself that she could find someone else if she had to. Maybe it was simply that she'd been drawn to the intrigue of being with a handsome stranger.

It really didn't matter why she'd done it. The fact was, Katie had slept with someone who wasn't Keith. And there was one thing that Katie could not ignore no matter how hard she tried: She had no one to blame for her actions but herself.

But there was no time for her to think about any of that now. She had to get back to the brownstone before she missed the weekend curfew! Without even looking back, Katie grabbed her hat and coat and darted out of the room. As the door closed behind her, Katie hoped that she had left the whole experience behind her. But she knew that wasn't possible; deep down, Katie knew she would never completely forget Jackson. He was a nice guy. It wasn't his fault that he just wasn't Keith.

It didn't take long for Katie to find a cab—taxi drivers usually hovered around hotels, searching for tourists who needed a ride. "Eightieth and Amsterdam," she told the driver as she settled into the backseat.

As the taxi traveled through Central Park, Katie could feel herself starting to cry. She'd never done anything like this before. In fact, until today, Keith was the only guy she'd slept with—or even kissed for that matter. He'd been her boyfriend forever. And now she'd betrayed him. Katie wasn't sure she'd ever be able to face Keith again.

Katie's shame burned deep within her. She'd just done something really, really stupid. What had possessed her to agree to take a hotel room with Jackson? She'd only known him for a few days. He could've been crazy or something. She could've been hurt—or even worse.

Well, at least they'd practiced safe sex. She could still hear Jackson's laughing voice as they'd stopped in the drugstore on the corner to buy condoms. "Hey honey, I know the drill," he'd said before she could even bring up the subject.

The thing that upset Katie most was that there had been no love between her and Jackson. It was simply sex—just like what went on between any of the horses on her uncle's ranch. The experience left Katie feeling hollow inside. Suddenly she missed the feeling of Keith's strong arms around her, and the way he managed to look right through her and into her soul during their most intimate moments.

Katie sighed sadly. After her last conversation with Keith, about Christmas vacation, Katie had a sick feeling that she would never feel the safe, comfortable sensation of being in his arms again. So where did that leave her now? Was her whole life going to be one meaningless relationship after another? Katie couldn't help but wonder if she'd made the right decision by staying in New York.

When the cab pulled up in front of the brownstone, Katie paid the driver and raced up the steps. As she turned her key to open the heavy front door, she glanced at her watch. Whew! Ten minutes to spare.

The brownstone was silent as Katie walked in. Most of the girls were probably asleep already. As Katie walked to her room, she said a silent prayer that Daria would be fast asleep like everyone else. Katie didn't even feel like facing her friends right now—she certainly didn't want to have to talk to Daria.

But Katie's prayers were not answered. When she entered the dorm room, there was Daria, wide awake, studying her Business of Music textbook. Daria glanced at the clock as Katie walked into the room. "Well, you cut it close," she muttered. "I thought maybe you'd caught the next red-eye back to cattle country. Where've you been, anyhow? The phone's been ringing off the hook. I've been playing secretary for you all night. And I'm telling you right now, that's not the way things are going to be around here. I have my own life, y'know."

"Sorry," Katie apologized. Although the barrage of phone calls hadn't been her fault, she was trying to avoid a confrontation at all costs.

"Your dad called, your brother called from college,

your friend Lyndsey called, and Keith called—three times," Daria snapped in her heavy Chicago accent. "He said you should phone him back before you go to bed tonight, and I sure wish you would. I have a feeling he's gonna keep calling all night until you do. Frankly, I'm sick of hearing his voice. I need some rest."

At the very mention of Keith's name, Katie exploded into sobs.

"Sheesh," Daria exclaimed, rolling her eyes in disbelief. "That's a new one. Now that dumb cowboy's making you cry before you speak to him!"

Chapter 8

Christmas was only a week away, but you'd never know it from the atmosphere at the Omega brownstone. Ever since Eileen's first critiques, the girls had been working overtime, focusing their attention on improving their performing skills while trying to keep up with their general studies as well. Tree trimming and caroling just didn't fit into the schedule.

But finally Alyssa couldn't take it any longer. She grabbed Melanie, Serena, and Janine and literally forced them to take a few minutes off to visit the Christmas tree salesman who'd set up shop on the corner of Seventy-ninth Street and Columbus Avenue, outside the Planetarium. The girls pooled their money and bought a small tree, which they placed in the lobby of the Omega Talent brownstone.

"This tree's pathetic," Melanie moaned as she stuck a shoelace through the hole in one of her old CDs to create a makeshift ornament. "It's so small. It reminds me of the scrawny tree from that Charlie Brown Christmas special they show on TV every year."

Serena frowned. "Don't be such a party pooper, Melanie," she also moaned. "It was all we could afford. Besides, even little Christmas trees deserve a home."

Melanie rolled her eyes. Sometimes Serena's bizarre relationship with inanimate objects amazed her. Like that ratty old stuffed animal she slept with sometimes . . .

"I like it," Janine declared as she walked out of the office carrying four packages. "And I think it gives the place some holiday atmosphere." Janine added the packages to the piles already gathered under the tree. "These just came in UPS delivery. I think one's for you, Serena. And the little one's from your dad, 'Lyss."

"Who's that huge one for?" Serena asked.

"Wait, let me guess. It's from Prince William to our little princess, Hannah," Melanie teased.

Janine shook her head. "Nope. It's from Katie's dad. You know they always do things bigger in Texas."

"Well, I can see that Santa hasn't delivered what I asked for yet," Janine said, playfully scanning the pile of packages.

"How can you tell?" Serena asked her.

"Because I asked Santa to send me the perfect guy, and not one gift under that tree has airholes in it."

Just then, Daria walked into the lobby and headed straight for the tree. She scanned the CD on one of Melanie's homemade ornaments. "Slayer, huh?" she remarked, looking at the label on the CD. "How quaint, an Ozzfest Christmas."

Melanie looked curiously at Daria. She was surprised that the girl even knew a band like Slayer existed. But Mel wasn't caught so off guard that she couldn't respond to her. "You have a problem with that?" Melanie asked. She didn't even stand up, but the look in her eyes was threatening enough.

Daria took a deep breath, rolled her eyes, and muttered a disgusted, "Whatever," as she headed up the stairs toward her room.

"What's with her?" Alyssa asked as she ate a few kernels of popcorn from a bowl on the floor.

"Hey, that popcorn's for stringing and hanging on the tree."

"Okay," Alyssa agreed as she swallowed the few kernels left in her palm. "Now, I repeat, what's with Daria?"

"I didn't notice anything unusual," Melanie said. "She still can't appreciate good music."

"Come on, you know what I mean," Alyssa insisted. "She's even more disagreeable than usual."

Serena pointed down to the pile of gifts under the tree. "I think the problem is that there're no gifts down there for her," she suggested.

"You mean the great legal team hasn't sent their darling daughter a gift yet?" Melanie asked. "Bummer."

Janine nodded. "I hate to say it, but I actually feel bad for Daria. It's like her parents barely remember they have a daughter."

"Well, if Daria were your daughter, would you want to remember?" Melanie joked.

"I'm serious, Mel," Janine said.

Melanie softened slightly. After all, even when her mom was at her worst, before she had spent that time at the rehab center, she'd always remembered to get Melanie something for Christmas. And no matter how small those gifts may've been, Mel had cherished every one of them. "Well, at least we've all gotten her something," she said. "She won't be completely left out on Christmas morning."

Just then Hannah came bounding down the stairs. When she saw the other girls she clutched the huge leather tote bag she was carrying tightly. That subtle action was not lost on Melanie. "Don't worry, Princess, no one's gonna steal anything from your bag," Melanie assured her.

"Huh?" Hannah asked with genuine confusion.

Melanie snickered. "Never mind."

"Where are you off to?" Serena asked her, trying to keep Hannah and Melanie from arguing . . . again.

"Oh, just some last-minute Christmas stuff," Hannah replied quickly.

"Well, don't forget, we've limited these gifts to ten dollars each," Alyssa reminded her.

Hannah smiled with just a touch of mystery in her dark eyes. "I know, Alyssa," she assured her. "And I think you guys are really going to love what I have for you."

"Well, that sounded promising," Serena said as Hannah ran out the door. "I think it's safe to say that everyone around here—except Daria, maybe—is getting into the Christmas spirit."

"Not Cass," Janine told her. "I think she's really dreading spending the holiday with her mother."

"Wouldn't you?" Melanie asked. She was still angry at Alana Morgan for convincing Cass to drop out of the number that she, Hannah, and Cass had put together for the PCBS Fall Showcase. "That woman is a total witch!"

"I know," Janine agreed. "I'm Cass's roommate, remember? You should hear the messages she leaves for Cass. She calls constantly, telling her that she's arranged special classes for Cass at dance studios, or for meetings with fancy diction coaches. She doesn't leave Cass with a moment to herself."

"She's controlling, all right," Alyssa agreed. "She reminds me of a drill sergeant. And poor Cass has no choice but to follow her orders."

Janine giggled. Somehow conversations with Alyssa always seemed to go back to the military.

Melanie glanced down at her watch. "Oh man, it's after five!" she moaned. "I was supposed to meet Sonia ten minutes ago for some extra work on that new dance. Gotta go!"

As Melanie sprinted off toward the dance studio, Serena sighed. "So much for Christmas spirit," she remarked.

Self-Expression Journal Entry

I've been sitting up here in my room all afternoon. I heard the other girls downstairs laughing and decorating a tree, but I didn't want to join them. I don't feel very Christmasy right now. And I didn't want to bring everybody else down.

I got a call from Lyndsey last night. She told me Keith is going to Sue-Ann Sims's Christmas Eve party. Her family throws the party every year, and we were always invited, but Keith never wanted to go until now. He always said that big parties weren't what Christmas was about. But I guess he's changed his mind about that.

I guess he's changed his mind about a lot of things.

The weird thing is that even though he's practically glued to Sue-Ann these days, Keith keeps calling me. He says he still loves me, and he hopes I'll come to my senses soon. I almost dread hearing his voice on the phone now. And that makes me even sadder than thinking about Keith at Sue-Ann's house.

I sent him a really nice present, anyhow — a Fossil watch that he's wanted for a long time. But there's still no package from him for me. I can't help but check every time there's a delivery, even though I've kind of given up hope.

Besides, the gift I'm waiting for can't come from Keith. Nobody can get it for me. That's because all I really want for Christmas is for my period to come.

That's right — I'm already a week late. And I've

never been even a day late before. Not in my whole life. So I'm starting to get really scared. I know Jackson and I were really careful, but condoms aren't 100 percent safe. How could I have been so stupid?

Jackson's called a few times and left messages on my machine. But I haven't called him back. I just can't talk to him about this. I don't think I ever really want to see him again. I know Daria must wonder why I've been screening all my calls lately, but that's just too bad. I don't owe her any explanations.

I'm so confused. The only thing I know for sure is that I don't have anyone to blame but myself. But if I keep thinking about this, I'll make myself nuts. So I'm going to sign off now.

Katie

Chapter 9

"I can't believe you're not going to spend Christmas Eve with your family!" Serena exclaimed as she watched Melanie pack one last sweater into her suitcase. "I'd give just about anything to be with my folks tonight, lighting the tree, singing carols by the fire . . ." Her blue eyes grew misty as she thought about what Christmas was like in her house.

Melanie scowled. "My family isn't exactly the caroling kind," she explained. "We're more the 'here's your gift, see ya later' type of family. Besides, Julia sorta planned this party, and I haven't had a whole lot of time to be with her since we moved into the brownstone, so . . ."

Serena bristled at the sound of Julia's name. Every time Melanie hung out with her best friend from her Brooklyn neighborhood, she came back a completely different person. At PCBS or in the brownstone, Melanie was a dedicated performer. Lately she'd even become more willing to let her softer side shine through. But after just a few hours with

Julia, Melanie returned to her old, angry self—the girl who thought the world had thrown her the lousiest break in the world.

But Serena could never tell Mel how she felt. Melanie would throw a fit if she ever said anything against Julia. "Well, we're gonna miss you around here," Serena had said instead.

Melanie nodded, but didn't answer. There was a side of her that really wanted to spend Christmas Eve in the brownstone. The girls who were staying behind had planned a great night. Since the dining staff had the night off, they were going to make their own Christmas dinner. Alyssa, a dedicated carnivore, and Serena, a total vegetarian, had argued over the menu, but they'd finally decided on turkey, stuffing, a tofu-stir fry, and some fried ice-cream concoction Janine swore was the most delicious dessert on the planet.

And that was just the dinner. Afterward the girls were going to open presents and stay up really late, just gossiping and giggling, because there were no rehearsals the next day. In the past, a slumber party would not have been Melanie's idea of a fun Christmas Eve, but lately the idea had seemed kind of appealing.

"Okay, that's it!" Melanie said as she squeezed her suitcase tight. "I'll see you tomorrow night."

Melanie walked down the hallway, dragging her suitcase behind her. When she reached the stairs, she bumped into Hannah, who was similarly loaded down.

"Well, off to that huge Christmas party at your

house?" Melanie asked with just a trace of bitterness in her voice.

"Yes, of course," Hannah replied quickly. In her mind she thought, I'm off to help my mom serve other people food at that big Christmas party. But of course she would never say that. Let Melanie think what she wanted. "How about you?" Hannah asked finally.

"Oh, I'm off to a party, too. But I don't think it's going to be anything like the uptown soiree at your crib. I'd say my Christmas Eve and yours are going to be completely different," Melanie supposed.

Hannah thought of the black dress and hideous white apron she was going to have to wear as she served the Aldens' phony, demanding guests. "You can say that again," she muttered under her breath.

"Okay, now I think we have to preheat the oven to three hundred fifty degrees," Alyssa told Janine.

"You can't do that," Serena interrupted her. "I'm roasting vegetables in the broiler. You can't work the oven and the broiler at the same time!"

"Well, this turkey takes a long time," Alyssa countered. "If we don't start it now, we'll be eating it tomorrow."

Janine poked at the turkey. "We'll be eating it tomorrow, anyway," she told Alyssa. "This bird is frozen."

"Of course it's frozen," Alyssa agreed. "But after we cook it . . ."

"You were supposed to defrost it beforehand 'Lyss," Janine said. "You can't cook a frozen turkey."

Alyssa held up a stained recipe book. "It doesn't say anything here about defrosting the turkey," she insisted.

Janine shrugged. "I think they assumed you already knew you had to do that."

Alyssa began to get upset. She hated when things didn't work out exactly like they were planned. When events were out of control, Alyssa seemed to spin out of control as well. "How should I know that?" she demanded of Janine. "I've never made a turkey before."

Katie wiped a bead of sweat from her forehead. "Well, I've gotta tell y'all, I'm glad the turkey won't be ready in time," she declared.

"What?" Alyssa, shouted her voice slightly climbing the musical scale as she grew more aggravated.

"I think I kinda screwed up this gravy," she admitted. "It didn't seem to be thickening, so I added a couple of extra tablespoons of cornstarch and . . ." Katie held up a spoonful of her gravy. It looked like gray, thickened oatmeal.

"Ooooh, gross!" Janine declared.

"Tell me about it," Katie admitted. "I knew I shoulda called my mother for her recipe instead of following those directions from *The New York Times*."

Beep! Beep! Beep! Suddenly alarm bells began ringing throughout the kitchen.

"What the . . . ," Alyssa began. She stopped as she realized that the kitchen was beginning to fill with smoke. "Something's burning!" she warned.

"Oh no! My roasted veggies!" Serena shouted as she flipped off the broiler, grabbed a pot holder, and pulled the tray of vegetables out. If Serena hadn't told the other girls they were vegetables, they never would've known. The roasted peppers and carrots were unrecognizable now—nothing but globs of blackened charcoal sitting on the silver metallic tray.

"Nice going, Serena," Daria sniped from her seat across the room. "Burn down the whole brownstone, why doncha?" She looked around at the other girls in the kitchen. "Well, this seems like a picture perfect Christmas Eve dinner—frozen turkey, lumpy gravy, and burned peppers."

That was more than Alyssa could take. "You've got a lot of nerve," she confronted Daria. "What've you done tonight?"

Daria rolled her eyes. "I've only been sitting here saving this dinner," she informed Alyssa. "You should be thanking me right now."

"What're you talking about?" Alyssa asked, not even attempting to mask the suspicion in her voice.

"Look, we're in New York, right? So we should celebrate Christmas Eve the way real New Yorkers do," Daria replied cryptically.

"Huh?" Alyssa replied.

Daria rolled her eyes again, as though Alyssa were the stupidest person on the planet. "I called in for dinner," she told Alyssa. "Hunan Cottage will be delivering a huge meal in about twenty minutes."

Daria looked around at the incredulous faces of her housemates. "Oh, and by the way," she added. "You all owe me fifteen bucks."

Hannah walked into the Aldens' huge kitchen and sighed. Christmas was supposed to be a time of good will and generosity, but you'd never know it from the crowd that had gathered in the living room of this Park Avenue apartment. The people out there were busy trading stock tips, or moaning about the horrors of rent-stabilization laws. Hannah had been serving hors d'ourves to the guests for almost an hour and she hadn't overheard one comment about the Christmas story, or church, or even Santa Claus. In fact, the closest any conversation had come to the true spirit of Christmas was when Mrs. Sklar had spoken to Mrs. Morton about her favorite charity. Of course she was only complaining about the food and service at the benefit ball last week—so Hannah figured that didn't really count.

"You look very tired, honey," Hannah's mother remarked. She kissed her daughter on the head.

Hannah looked at her mom. She looked tired, too. Hannah guessed that Mrs. Alden had been running her mother ragged all afternoon. That's what Mrs. Alden did every Christmas season. It was like she was making Hannah's mom earn every cent of that Christmas bonus she gave her each year.

"Look, they're going in to eat their main meal, and the caterers will do most of that serving," Hannah's mother told her daughter. "I think you can call it a night. Why don't you go call a friend and go out tonight?"

A sad expression washed over Hannah's face. How could she tell her mother that she really didn't have any close friends—that she'd been afraid to let anyone at the brownstone get to know her?

As Hannah looked into her mother's sweet, generous eyes, she felt a twinge of guilt. She knew that she really had nothing to be ashamed of. Her mother was a hard worker who wanted nothing but the best for her daughter. In fact, the only reason she'd started working for the Aldens in the first place was so that Hannah could live in a good school district when she was in elementary school. Mrs. Linden had become a maid in the hopes that her daughter wouldn't ever have to.

"I love you, Mom!" Hannah exclaimed suddenly, giving her a big peck on the cheek.

Mrs. Linden seemed surprised. "I love you, too," she assured Hannah. "Now, go on, get out of here. We'll celebrate tomorrow. I always have Christmas Day off. I'll meet you at church, and then we can have a nice lunch together back here. There'll be some amazing leftovers from tonight, I'm sure."

Hannah smiled. "That sounds nice, Mom," she replied. "Maybe I'll head back to the brownstone tonight. See what the girls are up to."

"Good idea. Before you go, Mrs. Alden gave me a whole pile of her old clothes and pocketbooks. They're in perfect shape—some even have the tags on them. But I can't really use them. See if anything fits you. Go back to that school in style!"

Hannah grinned. "Sounds great. Thanks, Mom."

As she watched her mom go back to work she couldn't help thinking that her mother, the maid, had more class in her little finger than any of those rich phonies in the dining room.

Melanie squinted as her eyes adjusted to the dark, smoky atmosphere in Tommy Moreno's apartment. The party was already in high gear when she and Julia arrived.

Eminem's "Slim Shady" blared out from the speakers Tommy had set up around the room.

"Now, this is music," Julia told Melanie as she started to bop up and down to the rap beat.

"He's good," Melanie agreed. "Although I'm not so sure I like all of his lyrics. He's kinda anti-woman."

Julia gave her a dirty look. "Well, at least he has a message—unlike those charming Omega groups out there."

Melanie didn't answer. She had to admit that in the past she hadn't been a huge fans of the love songs Eileen Kerr's pop bands had spouted. But Melanie had a feeling that No Secrets was going to be different. At least she hoped so. Already their look was different. No matter which of the eight girls Eileen eventually would choose, there would be more of an edge or an attitude to the group. Other than Serena, there wasn't a total Suzie Sunshine among them. But Melanie knew that explaining that to Julia was pointless.

"Hey, baby . . ." A tall boy with burning brown eyes came over and placed his arm around Julia. "I've been waiting for you all night."

"Sorry, I had to wait for my uptown girl over here to make her way to Brooklyn," Julia apologized as she flirtatiously twirled her long black and electric blue hair around her finger. Then she turned to Melanie. "You remember Jagger, don't you?"

Melanie searched her memory. She had a vague memory of this guy from elementary school—only his name wasn't Jagger then. It had been Paul. And back then he was more likely to have a calculator in his shirt pocket than the cigarettes he was now toting around.

"Melanie Sun. Well, haven't you grown up," Jagger remarked as he looked Melanie up and down.

Melanie didn't like a guy looking at her that way. "Hey Paul," she replied, making sure to use Jagger's given name. "I haven't seen you since you peed all over the cafeteria floor in second grade. Didn't your mommy have to come to school and bring you a clean pair of tighty whiteys?"

Jagger bristled at the use of his real name, and the way Melanie had brought up his totally nerdy past. He turned away from her and smiled seductively at Julia. "Wanna a beer?" he asked her. "Or maybe a shot of tequila?"

"Are you trying to get me drunk?" Julia giggled coyly.

"Hey, whatever it takes," Jagger told her.

"Beer's fine," Julia agreed. She turned to Melanie. "You want anything, M?"

Melanie shook her head. "No thanks."

"I'll be back in a flash," Jagger assured Julia as he walked off toward the keg in the back of the room.

"What're you doing with that loser?" Melanie asked Julia.

"He's not a loser," Julia argued. "And what was all that crap about second grade, anyway?"

"That's the last time I saw him," Melanie said, feigning innocence. "He doesn't go to our school. Where does he go?"

Julia stared into Melanie's brown, almond-shaped eyes. "You lost the right to call Hell High 'our school' when you moved on to that fancy boarding school in Manhattan," she informed Melanie. "But just so you know, Jagger dropped out two years ago."

"Oh, that makes him a real good catch," Melanie replied sarcastically. She watched Jagger work his way toward the keg. As he lifted his arm she could see a large tattoo on his bicep. It looked like a black rose lying beside a bloody dagger. Melanie gasped. That was a gang symbol.

"Look Julia, I don't want to freak you out or anything, but I think Jagger's in The Fears," Melanie told Julia gently.

Julia snickered. "Now tell me something I don't know."

"But Jules, that's a gang!" Melanie exclaimed.

"Again, something I don't know?"

Melanie didn't know what to say. Julia was hanging around with a gang member. "You're not . . . ," Melanie began.

"Relax, I'm not in a gang," Julia assured her.

"That's good," Melanie said. "But Jagger is. I'm worried about you."

Julia rolled her eyes. "Oh, please. Wake up, girl! There isn't anyone around here who doesn't need some sort of protection. The Fears are like a family to Jagger. They take care of each other."

"But Julia, a gang? You know what those guys are about."

"Can I help it if I like a little danger in my life?" Julia shot back. "Look, don't you come down here and criticize me. You left, remember? I've still gotta make my life work down here. You're living your life the way you want to—taking the safe road. I'm living my life the way I want to."

Melanie couldn't believe it. "I don't think of my music as safe," she argued. "I take chances."

"Oh, that'll end soon," Julia snarled. "I mean, after a while, you'll be one of those brainwashed little Omega Kewpie dolls, and all your edge will be gone."

"That's not true," Melanie argued. "I'll always be true to myself."

"Okay, I'll give you that," Julia acquiesced. "The question is, who are you?"

Melanie didn't have an answer for that one. Lately she'd been a little confused. Living in the brownstone with so many different types of girls had exposed her to a lot of new influences, musical and otherwise. She felt like she was growing in all sorts of directions. And maybe Julia sensed that Melanie was growing away from her.

"Look, if you can't accept Jagger and me, maybe you'd better leave. 'Cause I'm gonna be hangin' with him tonight," Julia told Melanie straight out.

Melanie looked around the room. Half the guys were drunk already. Couples were making out—and actually going a lot further than that—right in the middle of the crowd. Two years ago that would've seemed exciting to Melanie. But right now it just seemed ridiculous. These people were wasting their lives. That wasn't where her head was at. "Look, I think I'd better split," Melanie told Julia. "I just don't . . ."

The hurt and abandonment in Julia's eyes was unmistakable. But she refused to let Melanie know how she felt. "You just don't fit in here anymore," she said, finishing Melanie's thought. "Don't let the door hit you on the way out."

"I'll call you," Melanie said softly as she turned to leave.

Julia nodded. "Yeah. Sure, M. Sounds cool."

Chapter 10

Cass was out of breath as she opened the heavy brownstone door and walked into the lobby. She looked around but didn't see anyone. She sniffed at the air. Yech. What a stench. Sort of like a combination of smoke and lo mein noodles. "Anybody home?" she called out into the house.

"Back here!" Alyssa called from the kitchen. "Is that you, Cass?"

Cass wandered into the kitchen. "What a mess!" she exclaimed. "What happened here?"

Katie laughed. "You wouldn't believe it if we told you. What are you doing here? I thought you were at some big producer's party."

"Oh, I was. And it was awful. I snuck out while my mom was busy networking for me. She's gonna kill me when she realizes I left."

Janine smiled. She knew how much guts it had taken for Cass to deceive her mother. That party must've been just awful. "Hey, you want some chicken lo mein?" she asked.

Cass didn't say anything at first. Then she smiled and answered, "Maybe just a little bit. I'm still sort of full from dinner, but I always have room for lo mein."

Janine had a feeling that Cass hadn't actually eaten any dinner. But she didn't say a word.

Not long after Cass, Melanie arrived back at the brownstone. By then, all of the Chinese food had been scarfed down by hungry teenage girls. "You didn't even save me a noodle!" Melanie exclaimed, laughing as she threw down her suitcases.

"We didn't really expect you back so soon," Serena apologized.

"Relax, I was kidding," Melanie assured her.

"Why are you here?" Alyssa asked finally. "I thought you and Julia were going to show Brooklyn how to have a good time!"

"Oh, well, the party wasn't really all that happening, so I headed back here," Melanie answered. "Besides, I wanted to open my presents."

Just then Hannah came racing into the kitchen. "Hey! I heard that. You can't open those presents without mine," she insisted. Without even stopping to take off her coat and hat, she ran up the stairs to grab the gifts she'd made for her housemates. "Meet me by the tree!"

"What's she doing back here?" Daria asked.

"Don't bother asking. She wouldn't tell us, anyway," Melanie replied as she stood and headed out of the kitchen.

Hannah came down the stairs carrying seven identical long, thin boxes.

"Hey, they're not Tiffany blue," Melanie commented.

"You guys said ten dollars, so I stuck to that," Hannah assured her as she handed one box to each of her housemates. She looked around at the others. "Well, don't just stand there, open the gifts!"

The others looked at Hannah with surprise. Hannah was not usually this effusive, or happy.

"All right," Serena agreed. She tore open the box. Inside was a dark black, hand-knit scarf. At the edges, knitted right into the scarf, were the words NO SECRETS. "Whoa! This is soooo cool!"

"What'd you do, hire some poor child laborers to make these?" Daria asked dryly as she pulled her scarf from its box.

Hannah ignored her. "I made them. Each one," she told the others proudly. "I've been carrying around the yarn in that big tote bag all month long."

Melanie thought back. No wonder Hannah had clutched the bag so tightly when she'd run into the girls the other day. She hadn't wanted to let the girls know what she was making.

"Wow! This is awesome! Thanks, Hannah," Janine told her. "It's gorgeous. And no matter who makes the final band, we'll all have these scarves as mementos of our time here together."

"That was the plan," Hannah agreed.

"Okay, everybody, open mine next," Serena begged as she began handing out gifts to the other girls.

"So you knit these yourself, huh?" Melanie

whispered appreciatively to Hannah. "Princess, you're full of secrets, aren't you?"

Hannah nodded. "You have no idea," she assured Melanie.

Well, this Christmas was definitely ho ho ho-hum. It wasn't bad enough that I had to spend Christmas locked up in this brownstone prison with seven total losers. To make it worse, my parents didn't even bother to send a gift on time. My package didn't arrive until yesterday——the day after Christmas. So I had to just sit there while the rest of them opened gifts from home.

The package was from Saks, naturally. And the sweaters inside really were beautiful——especially the rust-colored cashmere. The only problem was they were about two sizes too small, and from the preteen department. I hate to upset my parents, but I moved on from there about five years ago. Of course it's hard to blame my 'rents for the sweaters being the wrong size, since I'm pretty sure they didn't exactly go traipsing out into the cold Chicago winter to shop for me.

But the least they could've done was tell the personal shopper at Saks my correct size. If they didn't know my size, all they had to do was e-mail me for it. Now I have to find a free minute to go to Saks and exchange the sweaters. And when am I supposed to do that?

Anyway, there're only a few more days until New Year's Eve. At least that should bring a little excitement. The other girls are heading down to Times Square for the night, and I guess I'll go along, too. I figure it has to be better than hanging out here the way we all did on Christmas Eve.

But until New Year's, it's business as usual at this brownstone. Everyone is working so hard to make the group. I hate to admit it, but they're all pretty talented. And that's going to make it tougher on me. Not that I'm not as talented as they are. It's just that things would be so much easier if one or two of them were knocked out or dropped out of the competition.

Since I can't depend on that happening, I'd better sign off here and get down to the gym. Joseph wants me to be able to do thirty push-ups without stopping by Friday. Give me a break! Now how is that going to turn me into a pop star?

DARIA

Chapter 11

Katie clutched the brown paper bag tightly as she ran inside and dashed up the stairs to her room. She peeked cautiously in the door before entering. What a relief. For once, Daria wasn't there.

Katie shut the door and plopped down on her bed. Then she opened the bag and pulled out the long, white, rectangular box inside. Tears welled up in her eyes as she saw the bright red letters on the box: EARLY PREGNANCY DETECTION.

Katie had been in a state of denial for at least a week now. She kept hoping that the next day would be the day her period came. But that never happened. Now here it was December 31, and Katie just couldn't face the New Year without knowing.

Katie opened the box and began to read the directions inside. Damn! She had to take the test first thing in the morning. That meant she'd have to wait a whole other sleepless night.

Suddenly Katie heard Daria's heavy footsteps in the hallway. It was easy to tell it was Daria without even having to look, since she walked on her heels. Katie placed the pregnancy test back in the brown paper bag, threw open one of her desk drawers, and tossed the test into the drawer. She slammed the drawer shut just as Daria entered the room. "Hey, Daria," Katie greeted her roommate. Her jolly tone was forced and phony.

"Hi . . . ," Daria replied with a touch of doubt in her voice. "What's up?"

"Nothing," Katie said. She tossed her head slightly so her blond ponytail bounced up and down.

Daria didn't say anything else. She went into her closet and came out holding a pair of slightly worn jazz shoes.

"Going to rehearse a little before we head over to Times Square?" Katie asked her, trying to seem nonchalant. There was no way Katie wanted Daria to suspect there was anything wrong in her life.

"No, I'm actually off to hunt in a safari, " Daria replied sarcastically as she dangled the jazz shoes in Katie's face.

Katie let out an affected giggle. "That's so funny," she mumbled nervously. "I mean, of course you're going to rehearse. Where else would you be going?"

Daria looked strangely at Katie. "Are you all right?" she asked as she pulled her dark hair back into a bun.

"Of course," Katie assured her. "Why wouldn't I be?"

"I don't know," Daria replied. "I thought maybe that psycho boyfriend of yours called again."

Katie shook her head and frowned. At the very mention of Keith it became impossible for her to keep up the perky act. "Not since I called him the day after Christmas," she told Daria. Katie sighed. That had been the worst moment of her life. She'd called Keith on the private number for the phone he kept in his room, and she could've sworn she'd heard a girl giggling in the background the whole time she and Keith were talking.

Daria rolled her eyes as Katie's face dropped. "Now that's the Katie I've come to know," she remarked snidely. "Mopey and depressed."

As Daria closed the door behind her, she smiled to herself. Something was definitely up with Katie. Obviously, whatever the issue, it was something big; bad enough for Katie not to want anyone to know about it. Katie had thrown something in her desk drawer when she'd heard Daria come in. Daria was almost certain that whatever was in that drawer was the clue that would solve this little mystery.

"Are you sure we can get out of Times Square in time for curfew?" Serena asked Melanie as she pulled yet another warm sweater over her head. The weather was freezing outside, and Serena wanted to make sure she wasn't miserable the whole time she and her housemates were ringing in the New Year.

"I dunno," Melanie admitted. "But I think so. "Anyhow, we're all gonna be there—even Cass. Eileen isn't going to get rid of all eight of us, right? So if we're a few minutes late, it won't be any big deal."

"I sure hope you're right," Serena said doubtfully.

"But just in case, let's not go too far from the subway stop. I wouldn't want to have to fight the crowds to get to a train after the ball drops."

"I just hope we can get any spot at all," Melanie complained as she darkened the eyeliner around her left eye. "I was watching the news before, and they said people have been staking out their spots since eight o'clock this morning. That was four hours ago!"

Serena pulled three ski caps from her drawer and looked them over. "Which one do you like best?" she asked.

Melanie looked at the brightly colored caps, each decorated with a pom-pom on the top. The hats just screamed "out-of-towner!" Melanie knew that wearing any of those ski caps would make the naive Serena a walking target for pickpockets. She reached into her closet and pulled out a small, dark blue cap. "You want to wear this?" she asked Serena. "It'll go better with your coat than any of these."

"Didn't you just get that for Christmas?" Serena asked.

Melanie nodded. "Yeah. So don't lose it. But I wasn't going to wear it tonight, anyway. I was going to wrap this scarf around my head."

"Gee, thanks!" Serena exclaimed.

"Don't mention it," Melanie replied. "To anyone."

"I'll be down in one minute," Daria promised the other seven girls who were waiting in the lobby. "I just want to grab one more sweater."

"Hurry up, Daria, we don't want to be stuck next to a bunch of jerks," Alyssa shouted up the stairs after her.

Daria resisted the urge to tell Alyssa that she was already with a bunch of jerks. No sense getting in a fight just now. Quickly, Daria raced into her room and shut the door. But instead of reaching into her closet for a sweater, Daria went straight for Katie's desk drawer. The drawer was filled with pencils, erasers, and a few mushy love notes from Keith to his "Sug." But right on top was a plain brown paper bag.

Quickly, Daria picked up the bag and peeked inside. A huge smile appeared on her face as she discovered what was inside. "Now this is what I call a Christmas present," she muttered gleefully to herself.

Chapter 12

The air in Times Square was brutally cold. The wind had been blowing mercilessly ever since the sun had set. And still, the eight girls were out there, braving the cold like the millions of other partiers in the square. Janine opened the thermos of hot cocoa and poured herself a fresh cupful. As she wrapped her hands around the warm Styrofoam cup, she shivered slightly. "You know, the first year I was at PCBS I loved the cold weather. It was so different for me. But I'm totally over it now. Bring me some Miami heat!"

"You'd think you'd be the warmest of all of us," Daria told her. "What with that extra layer you have . . . ."

Janine took a deep breath. She refused to let Daria get to her, especially on New Year's Eve. Janine's mother had a superstition that whatever you were like on New Year's was how you were going to be all year. So Janine was determined to stay happy and confident. She forced herself to turn away from Daria and focus her conversation on Alyssa. "So did you say your folks are moving again?" Janine asked her best friend.

Alyssa nodded. "Mom called this morning. Seems Dad's taking a desk job for a while—at my mom's request. She's the one who gives the orders in our house. But the position is in San Diego, so they have to move again. The weird thing is, their move doesn't really affect me. I mean, I don't live with them anymore. I live at the brownstone. We all do."

"At least for now," Janine said.

"Stop talking like that. You have to think positive at all times," Alyssa commanded.

Janine nodded. Alyssa was right. She didn't want to have to think that this was probably the last New Year's the eight of them would be spending together. By this time next year there would only be four.

"Hey Cass, how'd you spring yourself loose from your mom tonight?" Melanie asked.

Cass grinned. "My mom has a date tonight. She didn't want me tagging along."

"You don't seem too sad about that," Hannah teased her.

"Not at all," Cass assured her with a big grin.

Just then, three college-age guys sauntered over to where the girls were huddled in a group. The boys seemed a little unsteady on their feet. As they grew closer, the girls could smell why. They smelled like a brewery. It seemed like these three had been drinking all night.

"Just another thirty minutes till New Year's," the tallest of the three guys informed them with a slight slur in his speech. He smiled at Serena. "Hey Red, I'm looking for someone to ring in the year with? How 'bout you?"

The look in Serena's eyes was one of absolute fear. She'd never come up against a drunken guy in such a crowded area before.

Melanie was angry. Who was this guy to freak her roommate out so badly? "Get lost," Melanie told him in her most menacing voice.

"Excuse me," the tall guy apologized with a slight hiccup. "I didn't mean to be rude." He pulled a bottle of whiskey from under his coat. "How 'bout a shot as a peace offering?"

Melanie thought about it for a minute. She was cold, and the whiskey would warm her up. "Okay," she said, taking the bottle from his hand.

"Are you nuts?" Serena asked her.

"Hey, it's New Year's Eve," Melanie reminded her. She held out the bottle. "Any other takers?"

Cass took the bottle from Melanie's hand. She raised it high and made a toast. "To freedom!" she declared. Then she took a long swig from the bottle.

Daria was standing beside Cass. She reached over and grabbed the bottle. "Maybe this will help me forget I'm stuck here with you guys," she said.

"Gee, thanks a lot," Katie snapped at her roommate. "And don't hog it all. I've got stuff to forget, too, y'know."

Daria moved the bottle out of Katie's reach. "Do you really think you should, Katie?" she asked, her voice filled with mock concern. She waited to make sure that all the other girls were listening before she added, "I mean, being in your condition and all . . ."

"Wh-wh-what are you talking about?" Katie stammered nervously.

All eyes were suddenly on Katie. She did her best to keep her emotions in check. She just couldn't let on about what was going on in her life. At least not here. Not tonight.

"What condition?" Serena asked Katie, finally.

"I don't know what she's babbling about," Katie assured Serena with a quick, exaggerated smile. "She's probably just drunk already." Katie didn't say anything else, but she didn't take a drink from the bottle.

Melanie looked over at Hannah. "How about you, Princess? Of course, it's not Moët champagne or anything, so maybe you don't—"

"Oh, shut up!" Hannah scolded Melanie. She grabbed the bottle from Daria. "Give me that!" she demanded as she took a huge drink.

"Don't look at me," Serena told the others. "I don't want to get anywhere near the stuff. It just makes me stupid." Serena blushed as she remembered the one and only time she'd ever had anything to drink.

"You can say that again," Melanie agreed. And she would know, since it had been Melanie who had had to see to it that Serena got home that night. "None for you, kiddo, it's hot cocoa all the way! Janine, pour her a cup of that hot chocolate."

Janine grinned. "Only if you pour some of that strong stuff in my cocoa. It could use a little kick."

"Man, Eileen would kill us if she knew what we were doing," Alyssa said as she took a sip of Janine's spiked cocoa.

"Well, she's not gonna know," Melanie assured her. "I mean, no one here's gonna tell her. It's just our little secret!"

By now the booze was taking effect. The girls were getting silly. They removed their warm winter hats and replaced them with silly party hats they'd bought from a nearby vendor. They screamed and blew noisemakers with the rest of the crowd as the news cameras scanned their area of Times Square. Melanie hopped up on the shoulders of one of the college boys and waved. "Hello, Mom!" she shouted into the news camera. The other girls from the brownstone began to giggle uncontrollably.

The third college boy smiled shyly at Cass. "I think we know each other," he said quietly.

"No, we don't," Cass assured him.

"But you look so familiar," he insisted.

"That's because she's spent many nights in your living room," Melanie teased. "You probably had your first fantasies about her."

Cass blushed. "Mel, cut it out!" she insisted.

"Huh?" the guy asked.

"She's Cassidy Sanders. Child actress extraordinaire."

"Whoa! I'm getting drunk with Cassidy Sanders from *The Kids Company!*" he exclaimed as he realized just who Cass was. "How cool is that?"

"Pretty cool," Cassidy teased him, giggling. She spun around wildly. "Except I'm not Cassidy Sanders from *The Kids Company* anymore. I'm all grown up." She stopped spinning. "I'm also a little dizzy."

"You're not gonna throw up or anything are you?" the college guy asked nervously.

"Not tonight I'm not," Cass assured him.

The boy looked strangely at Cass. That had been a very strange response.

"Don't worry, I'm fine," she assured him. But it sounded more as though she were trying to assure herself.

"Hey, you guys, it's almost midnight!" Hannah exclaimed. "They're counting down! Look."

The ball was in position to drop. Numbers began to flash across the huge TV screen in the middle of Times Square.

The girls all counted in unison. "Ten, nine, eight, seven, six, five, four, three, two, one! HAPPY NEW YEAR!"

"Shhhh," Melanie ordered loudly as the girls walked up the steps of the brownstone. "No laughing!"

"We just made it," Alyssa said, looking at her watch. "It's twelve twenty-seven. No one here broke curfew." She put her key in the lock and opened the door.

As soon as the girls walked into the lobby, someone flicked on the lights. The brightness was overwhelming.

"Well, welcome home, ladies," Candace said as she greeted them. The look on her face, however, was anything but welcoming. In fact, she looked furious. "Before you turn in for the night, Eileen would like to see you all."

"Now?" Hannah asked.

"Oh yes, right now," Candace replied.

"This can't be good," Janine murmured.

"Very perceptive, Janine," Candace agreed.

Chapter 13

Eileen didn't say a word as the girls piled into her office. She refused to even look them in the face as they sat down gingerly on her green leather couch.

Eileen reached her arm forward stiffly and clicked on her TV remote. Instantly the image of Times Square appeared on the screen.

As the news camera scanned the New Year's celebration scene, Alyssa felt a sinking sensation in her stomach. She knew right away what Eileen was so angry about. And from the looks on her friends' faces, they had figured it out as well.

Within seconds the eight No Secrets' candidates' faces came into full view. There was Melanie, perched high on that college guy's shoulders, screaming out, "Hello, Mom!" Right next to her Cass was spinning around like a wild windmill. Serena looked almost frightened as Daria took yet another a swig from a bottle in the brown paper bag.

As soon as the news cameras passed the girls, Eileen flicked off the TV. "What were you thinking?" she asked in a calm voice that was almost a whisper. Eileen was not one to yell. But hearing her sound so measured was more frightening than any loud lecturing might be. It was almost as though there were an explosion brewing inside her that she was afraid to let loose.

"As far as I know, the drinking age in New York City is twenty-one. That means that you all broke the law tonight."

Serena was about to assure Eileen that she hadn't had anything to drink, but she had a feeling Eileen wouldn't be interested in her correction at the moment. And her friends certainly wouldn't appreciate a comment like that, either.

"Not only did you break the law, but you did it on national television. Right now, you're only eight unknowns. But that might change, at least for some of you. And this is not the reputation I want for the girls in any of my bands. I'm not into that doctrine of 'any publicity is good publicity.' That's not what Omega Talent is about. Got it?"

Eileen didn't wait for a response to her rhetorical question. "Now, I have already invested an enormous amount of time and money into your training. But make no mistake: I will cut my losses and get rid of each and every one of you in an instant if anything like this ever happens again. No exceptions, no excuses. I will not tolerate any behavior like this from anyone in this room again. There are to be no scandals."

Eileen took a deep breath and checked the face of each and every girl to make certain that her message had gotten through. Then she nodded. "I suggest you all go upstairs now, before I change my mind and end this training program right now!"

She didn't have to say it twice. The girls jumped up from the couch and ran toward the stairs.

"What a way to ring in the New Year," Melanie moaned as she followed Serena to their room.

"Hey, at least we're still here," Serena argued.

Melanie let out a small moan. Why did Serena always have to look for the silver lining in every cloud? It was positively annoying sometimes.

Just before she reached the third-floor landing, Serena turned and headed back down toward the second floor.

"Where're you going?" Melanie asked her.

"Down to Katie's room," Serena replied. "I just want to ask her something."

Serena knocked quietly at Katie and Daria's door. Daria opened the door and shot Serena an angry look. "What do you want?" she asked her.

"I need to talk to Katie," Serena told her.

"Take a number," Daria replied. "You're the third person tonight to come looking for Katie. What's so urgent?" Her brown eyes sparkled. Daria knew exactly why the girls had all taken such an interest in Katie. She was, after all, the one who had planted the seed . . . so to speak.

"Never mind," Serena said. "Do you know where she is?"

"Check Alyssa's room." Daria said as she slammed the door rudely in Serena's face.

Serena raced down the hall and knocked on the door of the room Alyssa shared with Hannah. There she found Katie, Hannah, Janine, and Alyssa sitting on the floor. Katie was all red-eyed and crying into a handkerchief.

"So it's true, then," Serena stated simply as she joined them on the hardwood floor. "What Daria was saying, I mean."

Katie shrugged. She knew exactly what Serena was alluding to. There was no point denying it. "I don't know," she said simply. "I just know that I'm a little late."

"And you told Daria about it?" Serena asked with surprise.

"No, of course not," Katie assured her. "She was probably snooping around and found the pregnancy test I bought this afternoon."

"Did you take the test?" Janine asked softly.

"Nope. You have to wait for the morning," Katie explained.

"Well, forget that test," Alyssa told Katie, characteristically leaping in to take charge of the situation. "Let's go to a doctor and have it done right."

"I don't have a doctor," Katie weeped softly. "I've never even been to a gynecologist before."

Alyssa wasn't going to let a little problem like that ruin her plan. "Hannah, you live here," she said. "What's the name of your mom's gynecologist?"

Alyssa asked her. "We'll take Katie there."

Hannah could feel the familiar stress building in her body. The girls obviously thought her mother went to some fancy Park Avenue doctor. She couldn't let them know that in reality her mother went to an HMO center in Queens.

"Oh, it takes months to get appointments with him. And I don't even know if he's taking any new patients." She looked kindly at Katie. "Why don't you go that Teen Clinic on Forty-eighth Street? They do pregnancy tests there, and they can refer you to . . . well . . . whatever kind of doctor you need to see next."

Alyssa nodded. "That's a good idea," she acknowledged. "You know, Katie, even if you are pregnant—and we don't know that for sure yet— there are a lot of options . . . "

"Oh, I know," Katie assured her. "I've been thinking about them. And not one of them is really what I want. Besides, no matter which option I choose, I'm out of No Secrets. You heard what Eileen said. 'No scandals.' And a teenage pregnancy is a scandal no matter which way you look at it."

"Hey, does Keith know about this?" Janine asked her. "Maybe you should call him and talk it all over with him. You might feel better if—"

Katie shook her head and felt the tears beginning to flow again. "I don't think calling Keith would do any good," she told Janine.

"But he'd want to know. This is his problem, too," Janine argued gently.

"No, it's not. It isn't his . . ." The word stuck in her throat. "Baby," she added finally. Baby. She'd finally said the word out loud. And it hung there in the air like a dark rain cloud.

"What! You mean you slept with someone else?" Serena blurted out the words before she could stop herself. Her disapproval and surprise were evident. Immediately, Serena regretted saying anything.

Alyssa shot Serena a dirty look. "Relax, Serena," she ordered. "This is not something new in the universe. It has happened before."

"Not to me, it hasn't," Katie sobbed. Then she looked into the faces of her housemates. All of them, even the usually distant Hannah, seemed genuinely anxious to help her. Quietly, and ever so slowly, she began to tell them all about Jackson and the whirwind week they'd spent together.

As Katie spoke, no one else in the room even uttered a sound. No one passed judgment—even Serena managed to keep her personal feelings hidden deep inside. They just let her speak.

When it became clear that Katie had finished her story, Janine finally took the opportunity to reassure her. "Look, you may not want to call Jackson, and that's up to you. But you're not alone. We're all here for you. And no matter what decision you make, we'll back you up. It's gonna be okay, Katie."

Before Katie could reply, the girls heard a loud thud coming from the lounge. They leaped up and ran to see what had happened. Hannah was the first one to reach the door. She peeked in and let out a painful little cry.

There was Cass, lying still and motionless on the floor beside the couch. There was a pool of blood forming by her head. "Oh, my God!" she exclaimed.

"Quick, Janine, call 911!" Alyssa ordered. "Serena, you go get Eileen."

Janine ran and did as she was told. But Serena couldn't move. She was frozen with fear.

"Fine! I'll get her," Alyssa shouted as she dashed out of the bathroom and down the stairs. "Just stay with her. Don't leave her alone, whatever you do!"

Chapter 14

Eileen Kerr climbed into the ambulance and took Cass's hand. She smiled with relief as the weary girl slowly opened her dark brown eyes.

"What happened?" Cass murmured in a barely audible voice.

"Shhh. Don't try to talk," Eileen told her softly. "You passed out and hit your head on the side of the coffee table. But you're going to be just fine. We've called your mother. She'll meet us at the hospital."

Cass's face grew even paler. "No, not my mom," she insisted. "She'll be so disappointed."

"Don't be silly, Cass," Eileen replied. "Your mother won't be disappointed. She'll just be glad that you're okay."

Cass felt too weak to respond. But even in her dazed state of mind Cass knew that her mother would be anything but glad.

"Ms. Morgan, were you aware that your daughter has an eating disorder?" the young emergency room doctor asked Alana as she and Eileen sat side by side in the waiting area of the emergency room.

Alana looked nervously at Eileen, trying to figure out whether or not Eileen had been aware of Cass's strange eating binges. But if Eileen had been aware of the problem, her expression didn't show it. On the other hand, Eileen didn't seem surprised at the news, either.

"I don't think she does," Alana replied, trying to keep her composure. "Sure, she's a little thin, but that's just her metabolism."

The doctor shook his head. "She's not a little thin, Ms. Morgan. She's five foot eight and she weighs eighty-five pounds. She passed out from lack of food. And there are some signs of scarring in her throat, from the acid that comes when she forces herself to throw up."

"You must be mistaken, Doctor," Alana harumphed as she shook her head defiantly. "What are you, an intern?"

"No, I'm a resident here at the hospital," the doctor replied.

"Well, I think I should speak to someone with a little more experience. You've obviously misdiagnosed my daughter." Alana was panicking now. If Eileen Kerr really thought Cass had an eating disorder, she'd surely be thrown out of the running for one of the four spots in the band. And Alana couldn't let that happen. Not when they'd come this far.

"We have a social worker who specializes in

problems like Cassidy's coming to speak with her in a few hours," the doctor assured her.

"I didn't give you permission for that," Alana told him defiantly.

"No, Cassidy did," the doctor replied. "She wants to talk to somebody, Ms. Morgan. She understands that she's killing herself. And she wants to find a way to stop it. She needs your help now, Ms. Morgan. She needs you to be there for her."

Alana could barely think now. The doctor's words were ringing in her ears. Killing herself. This was horrible. And it was only made worse by the fact that Eileen Kerr was sitting there witnessing the whole thing.

"I've always been there for my daughter!" Alana shouted angrily. "How dare you accuse me of being anything but."

Eileen put a calming arm around Alana's shoulder. "No one's accusing you of anything, Alana. This isn't about you. This is about Cass. We're all on the same side. We just want to help Cass get well."

Alana nodded. "When can I see her?"

The doctor twiddled his thumbs nervously. "Well, the thing is, Cass doesn't want to see anyone right now."

"Are you telling me I can't see my daughter?" Alana demanded.

"Why don't you wait until the social worker arrives in the morning? She'll be here around ten."

"She's not coming until ten?" Alana asked anxiously.

"Well, it is New Year's Day. She's making a special trip in for Cass," the young doctor explained.

"Well, I should hope so," Alana told him. "After all, my Cass is a very special young lady."

The doctor nodded. "Do you want to go home and rest?" he asked kindly.

Alana shook her head. "I think I'll stay here," she replied.

Eileen looked at Alana. "Don't you think you might want to go home and change?" she asked.

Alana looked down at the black Vera Wang low-cut evening gown she was wearing when she'd gotten the call about Cass. It did look out of place in the hospital waiting room. "You're right, Eileen," she agreed. "It's kind of silly to sit here all night if they won't let me see Cass."

Self-Expression Journal Entry

I'm so scared. Seeing Cass on the floor, with all that blood, was like something out of a bad horror movie. I don't know how I was able to think so fast. I just sort of took charge, like I was on autopilot or something.

I would like to say that I wonder what's wrong with Cass, but I think I know. In fact, I think we all know. Everybody around here has always figured she had some sort of eating problem, but we didn't want to say anything. Nobody wanted to confront her. What it all comes down to is we were all so worried about hurting Cass's feelings that we almost killed her.

Everybody's shaken up right now. Nobody's sleeping—except probably Daria. She didn't even blink an eye when we told her what had happened. She just went back to bed. She even acted pissed off that we woke her up. I swear, ice flows in that girl's veins.

I hope Eileen calls soon! I won't be able to rest until I hear that Cass is all right.

Alyssa

They're all downstairs huddled by the door, waiting for Eileen Kerr to come in with some news. But not me. Frankly, I hope Cass has to go off to some eating clinic somewhere for a while. That'll make for one less competitor for me. And if Katie really turns out to be pregnant, that'll be two down, giving me an even better chance of making No Secrets. And considering how my dancing is improving and how much Candace likes my voice, I should be a shoo-in!

Boy, this is turning out to be one spectacular New Year's! Cheers!

DARIA

Chapter 15

Hannah knocked quietly on the partly open hospital door.

"Come in," Cass called, in a voice that seemed stronger than it had in weeks.

Hannah walked in slowly, carrying a small bouquet of daisies.

Cass smiled brightly. "Hey, my first visitor from the brownstone. How are ya?"

"I'm fine," Hannah assured her.

"Where's everybody else?" Cass asked.

Hannah knew exactly where Alyssa, Janine, and Serena were—at the clinic offering Katie some much-needed moral support. But Hannah figured Cass didn't need to be worrying about Katie just then.

"Oh, you know Melanie, if she has a day to sleep late, she goes for it," she said, not wanting to add that Melanie was so tired because she'd been up all night worrying about Cass like the rest of them. "And the others were out of the brownstone before I woke up," she continued. Quickly, Hannah struggled to change the subject. "You're sounding pretty chipper," she complimented Cass.

Cass pointed to the IV that was connected to her wrist. "It's all the nutrients in this thing," she explained. "Gives me some strength."

Katie nodded. "Eileen told us what happened. I'm glad you're going to get some help."

For a minute, Cass was silent. "You know, it felt kinda good to tell the social worker the truth this morning. I've been lying about my eating for so long, I forgot how freeing it felt to be totally honest."

Hannah turned away and stared out the window. She knew that Cass was only talking about herself, but the conversation was hitting pretty close to home with Hannah as well. Cass had practically had to die before she'd told anyone her secret. Hannah had to wonder what it would take before her secret was revealed as well.

"Anyhow, the social worker and I talked for hours this morning. And by the time my mom came by, I had the guts to tell her everything," Cass explained. "Of course it helped to have the social worker here to help my mom deal with the truth. It sort of came as a surprise to her."

"Oh, I think deep down your mom probably knew you had issues with food. I think we all did. We just didn't know how to help you, Cass."

Cass nodded. "I know. It's not your fault. And I'm going to get help. But it isn't just the food. You see, this morning, I told my mom that I want to live with my dad for a while . . . in San Francisco."

Hannah's face registered her surprise. She barely remembered hearing Cass mentioning her dad. "I didn't know you and your father even spoke," Hannah said finally.

"Sure, we do," Cass assured her. "We e-mail each other all the time. And he calls. He's just not as vocal or visible as my mom. But we've stayed really close, even though mom doesn't like to think about it."

"So, if you're dad's so cool, how come you stayed with your mom all these years?" Hannah asked.

"I was just a little kid when they split," Cass explained. "Back then, judges almost always gave primary custody to the mother. I saw dad on the weekends. But then, when I started to go off on locations for movies, I didn't get to see him as much, 'cause we were out of town. Then Dad got the job in San Francisco, and even though I was supposed to spend vacations with him, my mom always seemed to arrange it so I was working during those times."

"Didn't your dad try to see you?"

Cass nodded emphatically. "Of course, he did. All the time. But mom convinced him that my career was very important to me, and that if he loved me he would let up on insisting that she follow the custody decree to the letter. And I was always too afraid of hurting my mother's feelings to let my dad know that Mom was wrong . . . that I needed him."

Hannah sighed. She couldn't imagine being that afraid of her own mother. The entertainment business certainly had caused some real issues in Cass's life.

The entertainment business! Suddenly, an awful thought entered Hannah's mind. "But, Cass, if you move to San Francisco, then—"

"Then I can't be in No Secrets," Cass finished Hannah's thought. "I know. Actually, to tell you the truth, I'm kinda relieved about that. I think I might actually be through with show business. At least for now. I kinda want to see what it's like to be a normal teenager for a change."

Hannah laughed. "Oh, I've been there," she said. "It's nothing to write home about."

"Well, I wanna try it, anyway," Cass assured her. "And if I miss the biz, I can always try to make my way back in to the game."

"How'd your mom take that news?" Hannah asked, knowing full well how Alana had probably reacted to Cass's revelation.

"She wasn't thrilled," Cass allowed. "But it wasn't as bad as I thought. The problem is, she has primary custody of me. And since I'm only sixteen, it's up to her to give me permission to go live in San Francisco with my father."

"Is she going to do that?" Hannah asked.

Cass's face fell. "I'm not sure." Cass watched Hannah's eyes narrow with anger at Alana. She suddenly felt an urge to protect her mother's reputation. "Look, my mom's had a lot to digest today—no pun intended. Anyway, this is a lot for her. And maybe I should've waited to tell her, but the social worker said—"

"The social worker was right," Hannah assured Cass. "And your mom will see that, soon. How long are you in here for, anyway?"

Cass shrugged. "I don't know. At least until I'm strong enough to leave. And then we have to find a therapy program for me out in California. Otherwise, there's no way they'll let me go. They made that perfectly clear." Cass stopped for a moment and looked at Hannah curiously. "Y'know, I think this is the longest conversation you and I have had in two years that wasn't about singing or dancing or acting."

Hannah blushed. She knew she wasn't the most friendly of the girls. But she did have her reasons for keeping her distance.

"I don't know what's going on in your life that keeps you so quiet," Cass continued. "But you should open up more. Let the other girls see what I've seen today. Y'know, the real you."

Hannah didn't say a word. She knew Cass had no idea what the real Hannah Linden was like at all.

Katie sat in the waiting room, shivering with fear. Her face was pale white. Her heart was pounding so quickly, she was sure that everyone else in the room could hear it. As she looked around the clinic waiting room, Katie saw other girls with similar, strained expressions. She guessed they were waiting for the same test results she was.

Janine squeezed Katie's hand. She didn't have to say anything. The show of support spoke for itself.

"Katherine Marr," a tall woman with a stethoscope around her neck called out.

Katie raised her hand slightly. "Here," she replied quietly.

"Come with me," the woman said. As Katie walked over beside her, the woman introduced herself. "I'm Carol Loman. I'm a nurse practitioner."

"Hi," Katie said softly.

Carol smiled gently. "First timer, huh?" she asked.

Katie nodded. Her face turned red with a combination of fear, shame, and stress. "Yes, ma'am."

"It's not so bad," Carol assured her. "The first thing we'll do is take some blood and get a urine sample. Then Dr. Weiss will come in and examine you. You'll like her, she's very nice, and very patient. And I'll be there with you every step of the way."

Katie relaxed slightly. She was glad Dr. Weiss was a woman. Maybe it wouldn't be nearly as embarrassing.

Carol took out a chart and began to ask Katie a bunch of questions, like when her was her last period, and what form of birth control she used. Then Katie went into the bathroom to give Carol her sample. When she returned, Dr. Weiss was already in the room.

The actual exam wasn't horrible—at least not as bad as Katie had imagined it. And, like she promised, Carol was there the whole time to hold her hand, and even make her smile a little. When the exam was finished, Dr. Weiss smiled at Katie. "Get dressed and meet me in my office. We'll talk a little."

Katie nodded, hoping the doctor would volunteer a little more information. Maybe even answer the big question: Was she or wasn't she? But Dr. Weiss left the room without another word.

Katie threw on her sweater and jeans. She'd never dressed so fast in her life. But there was no time to waste. Katie wanted to talk to Dr. Weiss as quickly as possible. She got dressed so fast that even Dr. Weiss had to laugh when Katie knocked tentatively at her door.

"Wow! You didn't give me a chance to sit down," Dr. Weiss teased.

Katie blushed. "Well, I was kind of nervous, and anxious and—"

Dr. Weiss nodded. "Well, you can relax. You're not pregnant."

At first Katie didn't feel anything at all. She was numb. It took a minute for the good news to settle in. Then a big smile of relief grew over her face.

Dr. Weiss gave Katie a minute to digest the information she'd just received. The doctor had had enough experience with teenage girls to know that when they were stressed out, their reactions were often on a time delay. Once she was certain that Katie understood she was not pregnant, the doctor grew serious. She looked Katie in the eye. "But you still don't have your period. And that is a definite concern. There are several reasons why that could happen, but my guess is in your case it's stress related. Have you been under some sort of unusual pressure lately?"

Katie almost laughed out loud. Some sort of pressure. Talk about an understatement. How about auditioning for a new band, fighting with your boyfriend, and living with a total bitch—all at one time? Now that's pressure!

Dr. Weiss could read Katie's expression easily. "That's what I thought. You need to relax, Katie. Maybe some of those stressful situations can be remedied. And while you're trying to do that, I'm going to give you the names of some relaxation tapes you might want to purchase. And you could try a yoga class." She handed Katie a piece of paper with the names of some tapes on it.

"You did a good thing, practicing safe sex," Dr. Weiss continued. "And you should continue to use condoms when you have sex. But there are other birth control methods that, when used with a condom—"

"Oh, that's okay," Katie assured Dr. Weiss. "I won't be needing any birth control. Not for a while, anyway. I'm sticking to the safest sex of all—complete and total abstinence. At least for now."

Dr. Weiss didn't say a word. She simply pulled some brochures on birth control from her drawer. "Okay," she agreed. "But, just in case, give these a read. We're always here if you want to come back and talk about any of them."

Katie bounded out of the doctor's office and into the waiting room. She could tell that her friends were eager for her news, so as she walked into the waiting area, she gave them a big thumbs-up and a grin that was the size of the state of Texas.

Serena was the first to jump up and give Katie a big hug. "Oh, Katie! I'm so happy!" she exclaimed. Then she grew more quiet and serious. "Look, I'm really, really sorry about what I said yesterday. I mean, if you wanted to sleep with someone, it's not my place to—"

Katie shook her head. "No, you were right. Sleeping with Jackson was just plain dumb."

"Well, you can put all that behind you now," Janine assured her.

Katie wasn't so sure. "I don't think I'll ever forget this scare," she confided to the others. "I probably shouldn't. You know what they say, 'Those who forget history are doomed to repeat it.' Or something like that."

Alyssa nodded in agreement. "I think we'll all learn from this one, Katie," she assured her friend. Then she looked over at Janine and Serena. "Our work here is done, ladies. How about we stop by the hospital now and visit Cass? She's our next support mission."

"You guys go ahead," Katie told them. "I'll visit her tomorrow. Right now, there's something I need to do back at the brownstone."

When Katie reached the brownstone she rushed right down to Eileen Kerr's office. Sonia was sitting outside, going through some e-mails on the computer.

"Is Eileen in?" Katie asked.

"Sure, she is," Sonia said. "Let me just tell her you're here. You want to give me a clue what this is about?"

"Okay. Yeah, sure," Katie replied nervously. "Just tell Eileen that I have to talk to her about eliminating some of the stress in my life."

Chapter 16

Daria walked into her room in the brownstone and threw her hat on her bed. She glanced over toward Katie's side of the room. Daria was not completely surprised to find Katie packing her things into a large black suitcase. "What're you doing?" Daria asked, trying to hide her triumphant smile.

"What does it look like I'm doing?" Katie asked her. "I'm packing."

Daria nodded. "So it's true, huh? Well, considering the circumstances, you're doing the right thing."

"What's true, Daria?" Katie asked. "Considering what circumstances?"

Daria shrugged. "You know, the baby and everything."

Katie looked at her curiously. "What baby?"

Daria shifted her gaze to Katie's belly. "Your baby, of course."

"What makes you think I'm having a baby?"

Daria thought quickly. Katie never had actually told her she was pregnant. Admitting that she knew was like telling Katie straight out that she'd snooped in her drawer.

"I guess I just assumed, what with all your crying, and your mood swings, and the calls home to Keith . . . ," she began.

"Not to mention the home pregnancy test you found in my drawer," Katie accused her finally.

Daria feigned surprise. "What? How dare you accuse me of looking through your things! I would never . . ."

Katie smiled as Daria squirmed around in the verbal trap she'd set for her.

"Well, thanks for all your concern, but just for the record, I'm not pregnant. And I never have been," Katie assured Daria coldly.

"Then why are you leaving New York?" Daria asked. "Did the pressure finally get to you?"

"Oh, I'm not leaving New York," Katie assured her. "I'm just leaving this room. From now on, you've got this place to yourself. I'm moving in with Janine. It looks like Cass isn't coming back."

Daria grinned. Cass was out of the competition, and she was getting a whole room to herself! This was working out just great. Talk about a happy new year!

"As soon as I told Eileen about how you'd been snooping around in my desk and spreading nasty rumors about me, she moved me right away," Katie explained in a voice that sounded sweet but was touched with acid.

Daria's face fell. Katie had gone to Eileen and told

her everything. This was not good. Eileen had specifically warned Daria about back-stabbing. Katie's accusations were bound to count against her—big time! Daria glared at Katie. "You little witch! Why would you purposely try to make Eileen angry with me?"

Katie laughed triumphantly. "Oh, I have a million reasons," she assured Daria. "Where would you like me to start?"

Janine was sitting on her bed strumming her guitar, when Alana Morgan burst into the room with the strength of a hurricane. Without even so much as glancing in Janine's direction, Alana went straight to Cass's closet, pulled out her suitcase, and began throwing clothes into the open luggage.

"Hello, Ms. Morgan," Janine said sweetly.

"Janine," Alana replied in a sharp, impatiently brusque voice.

"Is Cass leaving?" Janine asked. "For good?"

Alana didn't even look up. She kept on packing as she spoke. "Apparently. At least that's what Eileen Kerr informed me of this morning. She seems to feel that Cass would be better off not being part of No Secrets."

"Well, I think that's what Cass feels," Janine corrected her. "At least that's what she told me this afternoon when I went to visit her."

"Cass is only sixteen. She doesn't know what she wants out of life," Alana asserted.

"I agree with you," Janine told her.

Alana was about to bark out an angry retort when she suddenly realized what Janine had just said. "You agree with me?" she asked tentatively. Alana sat down on Cass's bed and stared curiously at Janine.

"I do," Janine agreed. "Cass really isn't sure what she wants out of life. But I think she wants to take some time to figure it out."

Alana snickered. "With her dad in San Francisco. Oh, that'll be helpful," she said sarcastically.

"I think it will," Janine began. Then, before Alana could argue with her, she added, "Living like any other teenager may just convince her that she misses show business—that it's in her blood, you know?"

Alana looked curiously at Janine. She'd always thought of the girl as a bad influence on Cass. After all, Janine obviously didn't have the look you needed to make it in Hollywood, and she didn't seem to care. But the things Janine were saying now made a lot of sense.

"I think you have to at least give Cass the chance to see how the other half lives," Janine continued. "Maybe she'll like it, and maybe she won't. But if you don't give her permission to try, she'll only wind up resenting you in the end. And that would be awful, considering how much you've given up for her." Janine had purposely added that last line completely for Alana's benefit. Personally, Janine felt that Alana hadn't given up a thing—in fact, she'd forced Cass to give up a lot of her childhood to chase her own dreams. But Janine had to be diplomatic if she was going to help her friend. "Besides, this is a great opportunity for you," Janine continued.

"It is?" Alana asked curiously.

"Of course it is. You're an amazing agent. But you've been focusing solely on Cass. This is your turn to maybe start your own agency, and really get your name noticed in the industry."

The expression on Alana's face told Janine that her comments had had the desired effect. All Alana Morgan had ever wanted was to be noticed by big name entertainment types. Now Janine had suggested a way for her to do it.

"You know, that's not a bad idea," Alana admitted finally. "With my track record with Cass, I'm sure I can attract a talented group of young performers. And I definitely know how to sell them. Look what I did for Cass." Alana slammed the suitcase shut. She pulled a second piece of luggage from the closet, threw it on the bed, and began to open it. But she stopped. "I think I'll pack up later," she told Janine. "I haven't visited Cass at all today. I need to go over to the hospital."

"Great idea," Janine said with a smile. She knew perfectly well that in just those few seconds, Alana had already convinced herself that the agency idea was totally her own. And that was fine with Janine. She didn't want any credit. She only wanted to make sure Cass had the chance to get well, and to learn who she really wanted to be.

Chapter 17

Cass had been in the hospital for a week already, and Janine had gotten used to having a new roommate—sort of. Katie's mood swings were tough for Janine to handle—sometimes Katie was happy and at other times she was depressed and exhausted. Janine knew that it was all related to her problems back home, but she couldn't help wondering just how much longer Katie was going to be like this.

As Janine walked up the stairs toward the room she now shared with Katie, she could hear the Texan's voice blaring through the door. She figured Katie must be really mad. Usually she was more careful about keeping her phone conversations to herself.

"What do you mean it's not up to me to end it? If I say it's over, it's over. And as far as I'm concerned, this is the end of the road. You and Sue-Ann Sims are free to have a wild orgy in your daddy's barn for all I care!"

Janine sighed. Well, that explained Katie's loudness. She was obviously talking to Keith. And for once she wasn't letting him push her around. *Good for her.*

There was some silence in the hallway while Keith took over the conversation from his end for a while. But eventually, Katie's Texas drawl filled the air once again. And this time she sounded even more angry than she had before.

"Look, I tried doing this nicely. But you are making this *extremely* difficult. Accept it, Keith. **We are over.** And you're not the one who is deciding it. I am."

There was a little more silence. Then Katie slammed down the receiver without saying anything more. Janine waited a second and then knocked quietly on the door. "Is it safe to come in?" she asked.

Katie opened the door. Her face was flushed red with anger and the sheer excitement of the moment. "Was I that loud?" she asked, crinkling her nose slightly.

Janine nodded. "Oh, yeah. But I think there's some guy on Staten Island who still may've missed it."

Katie smiled. "It's just that Keith made me so mad," she admitted. "He kept saying that our relationship wasn't over until he said it was."

"I guess you shocked him," Janine said. "It's the first time he wasn't in control of things."

Katie shook her head. "That's not true. He didn't want me to come to New York, but I'm here. It just took me a while to realize that if I had the courage to do that, I had the courage to let go of a relationship that was dragging me down."

"I never thought of it that way," Janine admitted. "But you're right. You *have* stood up to Keith before."

"I guess he just always assumed that sooner or later he'd get me to come back and do things his way," Katie explained. "But I think he knows now that's not gonna happen." She smiled brightly. "I've moved away from Daria, and gotten rid of Keith. I've eliminated two big stresses in my life, just like Dr. Weiss told me to. We should go celebrate!"

Janine smiled and put a supportive arm around Katie. Somehow, Janine had a feeling that they hadn't heard the last of Keith or Daria. But Katie looked so proud of herself that Janine didn't have the heart to destroy her good mood. So she kept her thoughts completely to herself. "Sounds good to me," she said instead.

Serena was just walking out of the gym when she heard Melanie's distinctive keyboard playing coming from one of the studio practice rooms. She walked down the hall and peeked inside. Sure enough, Mel was right there, working out some riffs. She looked really focused. Serena didn't want to disturb her when she was in the middle of a thought, so she quietly tried to sneak off.

But before Serena could turn away, Melanie smiled in her direction. "I've got it!" she declared excitedly.

"Got what?" Serena asked her.

"That's just the chord I needed to end this song," Melanie told her. "You gotta minute? I want to try this tune out on someone."

Serena threw herself down onto a chair in the corner of the room. "I'm all ears," she told her.

A look of enormous concentration came over Melanie's face. She stared at the keyboard for a few minutes, collecting her thoughts. Finally she began to play.

The tune was a sort of rock-and-roll ballad. Like many of Melanie's songs, on the surface the lyrics simply told a story. But if you really thought about what what Melanie was trying to say, the words had a deeply profound message. In this particular case, the song talked about two friends who had grown up together but were rapidly growing apart. One friend was trying to build a bridge, while the other kept knocking the bricks away.

Serena didn't know a whole lot about Melanie's friends from her old neighborhood, but she had a feeling that the message in this song had its roots in her relationship with one of the girls Melanie knew in Brooklyn. It had to. Melanie always drew on her own life for inspiration.

As Melanie finished the last chord—the one Serena had heard when she'd entered the room—she looked over hopefully at her roommate. "Well, whaddaya think?"

Serena took a deep breath and measured her words carefully. "It's definitely got your signature sound, Mel," she told her. "You know, straightforward, and to the point. But it's hard for me say, y'know? I mean, we're all so wrapped up in this pop sound right now, and your stuff is kinda hard-edged. It doesn't even have a chorus or anything. It's just not where my head is right now. I wouldn't be a fair judge."

Melanie nodded. She knew Serena hadn't liked the song. But she would never come right out and say something like that. She was trying to be kind. Melanie couldn't help thinking that she would have been happier if Serena had just come out and said what she thought instead of dancing around the truth. At least that would've been honest. Melanie really respected that in a person. "Well, thanks for listening," Melanie murmured.

Serena stood up. "No prob. But I gotta run. Janine and I are supposed to study for a vocabulary quiz together in ten minutes."

As Serena left the room, Melanie stared at the keyboard. Although Melanie prided herself on never crying, she could feel a few tears suddenly welling up in her eyes. It wasn't anything Serena had said; Melanie had almost expected that reaction from her. It was more that there didn't seem to be anybody here who really understood her music. Julia had always known exactly where Melanie was coming from when she wrote her songs. It was their kind of sound—filled with the frustration and anger of growing up in a tough neighborhood while the rest of the world seemed to be flourishing around you. But lately Melanie and Julia didn't see eye to eye on a whole lot of things. In fact, they hadn't spoken since Christmas Eve. For the first time in a really long time, Melanie felt utterly and completely alone.

"Hey Melanie, did I . . ."

Melanie turned away from the door as she heard Hannah's voice. She certainly didn't want Miss High and Mighty to see her so upset.

"What's wrong?" Hannah asked.

"Nothing."

Hannah shrugged. "I just thought I heard you playing something. And it actually sounded kinda cool."

As she spoke, Hannah could feel butterflies forming in her stomach. Friendly conversations didn't come easily to Hannah. But she was determined to take Cass's advice. Hannah wanted to have friends. She didn't always want to be left on the outside looking in. And while she knew she couldn't let the others know the truth about her family, maybe—just maybe—she could let them get to know her. A little.

But as Hannah watched Melanie's face turn from sad to angry, she thought better of the idea.

"I'm not in the mood for your condescending jokes!" Melanie barked out at Hannah.

"I'm not joking. And I'm never condescending! You are!" Hannah cringed. This was not going well at all.

Suddenly, Melanie's tone changed. "You really like the song?" she asked nervously—not quite sure how to take this sudden change in Hannah.

"Yeah, I really do. Except—"

Melanie scowled. "I should've known there'd be an 'except' in there somewhere."

Hannah smiled. "I was just going to say that if you

want to present the song to Eileen, which is what I assume you had in mind . . ."

Melanie nodded slowly.

"Then, you'll have to work out harmonies for four voices. Eileen tends to frown on solo pieces in her groups," Hannah continued. "I think the chorus could be expanded, and maybe the bridge could be changed a little to accommodate a fuller sound."

Melanie didn't say anything for a few seconds. She was letting the idea settle in. Finally, she stared right into Hannah's eyes. "Are you saying you want to help me?"

"Not necessarily," Hannah replied. She took a deep breath. "Unless you want me to help you."

Melanie looked curiously at Hannah. She scanned her face, trying to see if Hannah had an ulterior motive in all this. But, like always, Hannah's face was completely void of emotion. Melanie couldn't help thinking that Hannah should play poker—nobody would ever be able to tell what kind of hand she held. Hannah kept her emotions hidden all the time.

But the more Melanie thought about it, the more she knew that Hannah was right. She would need to add some harmonies to the piece if she ever wanted it to be performed by an Omega band. And Hannah was a whiz at creating interesting harmonies. "Okay, I guess that might be okay," she agreed finally. "But, remember, it's my song! You're just helping with the arrangements."

At first, Hannah felt like walking away. After all,

Melanie certainly didn't sound grateful for her help. But then she remembered what Cass had said. Melanie didn't know it, but in some ways she actually was the one doing Hannah a favor, not the other way around.

"Of course it's your song," Hannah acknowledged. "Besides, who'd ever believe a girl like me could relate to lyrics like those. I mean, it's totally not my experience. It's more about your neighborhood than mine."

The words hung in the air for a minute, like a curtain separating the two girls. Hannah hadn't meant to mention anything even remotely related to her fabricated life, but it had slipped out. Things like that happened all the time to Hannah. It was like she sometimes forgot where the fake Hannah Linden ended and the real one began.

Surprisingly, Melanie didn't seem angered at all by the comment. "Seriously," she agreed. "This song is not Park Avenue."

"I know," Hannah told her with a sigh of relief. "That's what it makes it so authentic . . . so incredibly honest!"

Melanie seemed surprised at the way Hannah was able to see what she was trying to do with her lyrics and her music. Nobody other than Julia had ever been able to understand it in quite that way.

"Exactly," Melanie agreed enthusiastically. "That's what I was going for. Emotions that are raw, real . . . the total truth. Don't you think that the most important thing is to keep your art completely honest . . . totally about the truth?"

Hannah tried not to flinch. *Truth.* Funny how that word kept popping up lately.

It's really strange, but I feel like there's some sort of weird bond between Melanie and me. I mean, on the outside, nobody could look more different than we do. She's so dark and mysterious, and I look like . . . well, I look like Mrs. Alden. After all, I wear all her hand-me-downs.

But of all the girls here I think she's the one I really kind of understand. Maybe that's because underneath it all, we have a lot in common. We're both dealing with our homes, and trying to do more with our lives than our moms have. (Not that I'm putting down my mom or anything. She's sacrificed everything for me.)

The only difference is, Melanie has friends. Lots of them—here and in her old neighborhood. I've never really had a chance to make any friends. When I lived at the Aldens', I was never allowed to bring any other children over to play. Mrs. Alden was barely tolerant of me living there. She certainly didn't want any of my public school buddies coming into her pristine palace. And after a while, the other kids just stopped inviting me over. So I kinda got used to being alone. That's why it didn't bother me when I started spending most of my time by myself at PCBS and here at the brownstone.

At least I didn't think it bothered me. But when I was talking to Cass at the hospital, it seemed really nice to be hanging out with someone else. I'd forgotten what it was like to just have a conversation. I could just be her friend.

That's why I decided to take her advice. It wasn't easy talking to Melanie—at one point I thought she was going to bite my head off. But after a while it was fun. It was all about the music. Not about the tough girl or the princess, or any of that personality stuff. It was about what harmonies will work here, and how can we use notes to paint a picture and get the message across. It was exciting—like we were creating something really special!

The question is, will Eileen think the song's as special as we do? I know it would mean a lot to Melanie for Eileen to have the girls that wind up in No Secrets record her song. And for some reason, it's begun to mean a lot to me, too. It's like even if we don't make the band, we've left some sort of legacy or something. And that would be so cool.

Hannah

P.S. Ms. Lawrence, I know I keep writing this same thing in my journal, but please, please, please keep what I've written in here private.
Thanks.

Chapter 18

"You're lookin' pretty good!" Alyssa exclaimed as Cass walked into the lobby of the brownstone about a week and a half after her accident in the bathroom. Alyssa tried not to reveal what a lie that was. Cass actually looked exhausted, and scarecrow thin. But at least she was standing.

"Thanks. I'm feeling a lot better. But I still have a long way to go," Cass admitted. "Where's everybody else?"

"Rehearsing. Eileen had another one of her personal critique marathons yesterday, and I think she scared all of us. Every time we think we're doing better, she seems to find something new for us to work on."

Cass giggled. "She's tough, all right. But that's why No Secrets is going to be the best someday . . . " Her voice drifted off in a mournful manner.

"I'll bet you won't miss all the critiques," Alyssa mentioned, hoping to keep Cass's spirits from falling.

"I hope not," Cass said. "I mean, I don't know what I'll miss and what I won't."

"Life's full of surprises," Alyssa agreed. "Who knows what lies ahead for you in San Francisco?"

"That's what makes it so scary . . . and so exciting," Cass told her truthfully.

Just then Janine came bounding up the stairs. Her workout gear was covered with small ringlets of perspiration. "Alyssa, you were supposed to come get me when Cass arrived!" she scolded her best friend. "You're hogging her all to yourself." Janine smiled at Cass. "It's so good to see you up and around! I'd give you a hug, but . . ." She indicated the sweat marks on her clothes.

"Somebody's been working out," Cass acknowledged.

"Joseph said I had to work on my arms more. I've been lifting."

"Lifting is good exercise," Cass agreed.

Janine turned beet red. "I'm sorry. Maybe I shouldn't have said that. You probably aren't allowed to exercise or anything, right?"

Cass shook her head. "I'll be allowed to exercise soon. I just have to build up my strength. And I'll have to work on determining how much exercise is right for me. I was kinda overdoing it before."

The conversation was obviously making Cass uncomfortable. Janine quickly scanned her mind trying to come up with something to say that would make all three of them relax a bit. "There's been some weird stuff going on around here since you left," she told Cass. "For starters, Melanie and Hannah are working on arranging a song . . . together! And from what I hear, it was Hannah's idea in the first place."

Cass smiled. She had a feeling she knew why that had happened. "I don't think that's weird at all," Cass replied. "There's more to Hannah than you think."

"There'd have to be," Alyssa agreed. "I can't get a handle on that girl at all."

Cass shrugged. "Maybe you just have to try a little harder."

"Maybe," Alyssa allowed. Then she changed the subject. "What time's your dad getting here?"

Cass glanced down at her watch. "In a few minutes. I wanted a few minutes here by myself to sort of say good-bye. And to say thanks to you two again for saving my life. If you hadn't acted so quickly, I could have bled . . ." Her voice trailed off again as she imagined what could have happened had Alyssa and Janine not acted so quickly.

Janine put an arm around her. "But you didn't. And that's all that matters."

Cass smiled gratefully. "I really hope you guys are half of the final four," she said sincerely. "It would be great fun for you."

Janine looked carefully into Cass's eyes. For a moment she thought she saw a twinge of regret. "This is a good thing you're doing, Cass," she assured her friend. "You need to get well."

"You know, I'm not used to making decisions for myself. And boy, did I start with a big one. I'm leaving ʼy career, moving to a different city, and trying to reconnect with my dad—who I haven't lived with since I was a little girl." Cass sighed.

Just then the doorbell rang.

"Speaking of dad," Cass said excitedly, "that must be him!"

Janine walked over and threw open the brownstone door. A tall man with short dark hair that was slightly graying at the temples stood on the porch. There was no mistaking that he was Cass's dad. He had the same dark eyes, and the same strong chin. Janine was a little surprised to see him wearing a sport jacket and a tie, though. He looked so normal—like anybody else's dad might. Somehow, Janine had pictured Mr. Sanders to be dressed in jeans, with a long ponytail or something. Cass had told her all about how her dad was a hippie during the sixties.

Of course now Mr. Sanders was an English professor at a college near San Francisco. Obviously people changed as they grew up. Janine knew all about that firsthand. After all, look at how much she and the other girls had changed since they'd first arrived in New York City.

"You must be Mr. Sanders," Alyssa said, reaching out her hand and leading him in through the door. It was an obvious attempt to draw attention away from the fact that Janine was staring at Cass's dad with such curiosity.

Cass's father smiled. "Yes, I am." He reached a strong hand out. "I'm Dave Sanders. And you must be Alyssa. I love the purple in your hair."

"Thanks," Alyssa replied.

Dave turned his attention to Janine. "And you have to be Janine," he said with a grin. "I've heard so much about you—from Cass and her mother. Janine, I don't know what you said to Alana, but whatever it was, it worked miracles. I think she's actually excited that Cass is coming to live with me for a while." He gave his daughter a squeeze.

"Hey, let me get everybody else so they can say good-bye," Alyssa volunteered. "If you leave before they can see you, Janine and I are dead meat around here." Quickly she raced upstairs. From down below, Cass, her dad and Janine could hear Alyssa knocking on doors and calling the others to the lobby. Almost within an instant there was a stampede of teenagers racing down the stairs.

One by one the girls said their good-byes. Most of them had a secret message to whisper in Cass's ear, or an encouraging squeeze for her. But when it came to Daria's turn, there was an uneasy silence. Nobody ever knew how Daria would react in any given situation. And she'd certainly made no secret of the fact that she was happy to have one less competitor. Would she do or say something awful to Cass now?

But Daria surprised them all. She simply went over, gave Cass a stilted hug, and wished her "good luck in San Francisco."

The girls were amazed. Cass hugged Daria back with surprise. Everyone else watched, their jaws dropping with amazement.

Daria didn't acknowledge their puzzled stares outwardly, but inside she was laughing. She'd fooled them all into thinking she cared about Cass. And if she could fool the girls about her change in attitude, she could surely fool Eileen Kerr. And that was all Daria really cared about.

And then there was really nothing left to say. Everyone realized that it was time to say good-bye.

"Well, I guess this is it, then," Janine said, choking back the tears.

"Hey, it's not good-bye!" Alyssa assured her two, weepy friends. "We'll see Cass again soon. Like when No Secrets plays San Francisco!"

Cass grinned. Alyssa sounded so confident that she would be part of the band. "You should really take that positive attitude and bottle it!" she told her. "You'd make a fortune. I'd certainly buy a few cases for myself!"

"You don't need it," Alyssa assured her. "It takes a lot of self-confidence to know when you need a change in your life. I think what you're doing shows a lot of guts."

Cass stood a little taller. She'd never looked at it that way before. "I'll write you guys," she promised. "Of course it may take a few weeks. I have to get settled in my new room at Dad's place. And then I have to start school, and begin my daily sessions at a local eating disorder clinic, and—"

"Relax," Janine told her. "You don't have to write. We can e-mail each other, and call sometimes. I for one refuse to say good-bye. I'm just gonna say, 'See ya soon.'"

Cass nodded. Slowly she turned and looked up at her dad. "We've gotta get to airport, huh?" she asked.

Her dad nodded. "The cab's out front."

Cass smiled through her teary eyes. "See ya later," she said softly as she turned and walked out the door. The other girls followed her as far as the stoop, and waved as the cab drove away.

As soon as the cab that carried Cass and her dad had traveled out of sight, Hannah, Melanie, Daria, Serena, and Katie went back inside. There were rehearsals to attend, compositions to write, and dance classes to go to. But Janine and Alyssa stood outside for a minute, absorbing everything that had happened in the past few days. Cass was right: If they hadn't found her, she could've died. But she hadn't. Cass was a survivor. And now she was riding off toward a new life with her dad.

After a few minutes, the two best friends turned and headed back inside the house. From the moment they entered the lobby they could hear Hannah and Melanie arguing over a passage in Melanie's song. But the argument was different from the ones the two girls had had in the past. Sure, it was loud. But there was no name-calling or endless bickering. This was totally a work-oriented discussion.

"How weird is it that Melanie and Hannah are working together? I thought those two would never even *speak* to each other again after the PCBS showcase last month," Janine agreed.

Alyssa giggled, remembering how Melanie and Hannah had argued with each other until the very second the curtain had come up for their dance number. "I know. It's bizarre, all right. But it just goes to show you, there's no way to predict the future."

"I wish I could predict Cass's future," Janine mused. "Everything seems so unsure for her right now."

"Look, nobody knows what surprises lie ahead in their lives," Alyssa told Janine. "We don't know which four of us are going to be part of No Secrets, do we? I figure right now, Cass's future is as unpredictable as everyone else's. And that's all Cass really wanted—to just be like everyone else."

Janine waved her hands in front of her face like a mad fortune-teller reading a crystal ball. "Well, I know what my immediate future holds," Janine teased in her most mysterious voice. "A hot, steamy shower, followed by a not-so-exciting afternoon of working on my solo spot for that new song."

"Sounds like my day," Alyssa said, sighing. She thought for a minute about how ironic that was— Cass's leaving was going to change everything . . . and nothing. "I guess life goes on," Alyssa murmured as she followed Janine upstairs.

Self-Expression Journal

I know I don't have to write in this book anymore, but I think I'll keep it up for a while. When I write in this journal, I feel a connection to who I used to be. And although I had plenty of problems when I was at PCBS and at the brownstone, I don't want to lose the person I was there. I just want to get stronger — physically and emotionally.

It was hard saying good-bye to the others. I know that even though we vowed to keep in touch, chances are we'll drift apart after a while. It's like when you're on the set of a movie. Everyone gets so close because things are incredibly intense. You feel like everyone there is part of your family. But once the movie's over, you go back to your real life.

So, here I am, starting out on a whole new real life. I wonder what it's going to be like. I've never been to a regular school. Will the kids think I'm weird because I used to be on TV? Or worse, what if they only pretend to like me because they think I have connections? Is anyone there going to like me just because I'm me?

I think Melanie feels like I'm running away from my problems. At least that's the vibe I got from her when she came to visit me at the hospital. She seemed to find it so weird that anyone would want to give up a chance to perform. But, you know, I've been there, done that. And being in the business was never my decision. I think that's what Melanie doesn't get. She's always had to make all her own decisions. So no matter which way things go for her, she'll get the credit, or the criticism. My mom always took all the credit for my successes.

All I want is to be responsible for who I am and what I do. I guess that's why I don't feel like I'm running away from anything. I feel like I'm running toward something. I'm just not sure what. And that's what makes it all so scary, and exciting.

Cass

I swear I feel like Eileen Kerr has me under a microscope. Ever since Katie went and whined to her about me, Eileen's been totally on my case. If I even breathe funny she shoots me this look like I'd better play by her rules or it's all over. And she spent my entire critique this week talking about the fact that attitude was every bit as important as talent when it came to being a success. Now if that's not a total load of crap, I don't know what is. Musicians have always had attitude. It comes with the territory.

Still, I guess Eileen needed to say something. After all, she has to give each girl some sort of criticism. And my dancing and singing are better than anyone else's here. So I guess she had nothing else to talk about. Maybe she just wants to prepare me for life on the road. I won't always have my own room. Even Omega Talent performers have to share hotel suites once in a while.

Still, I know I'm gonna have to lie low and play by the rules until this whole thing blows over. But, hey, I can't help it if one of the girls trips herself up . . . can I?

One can only hope.

DARIA

Break out the bubbly! I finally got my period this morning! Dr. Weiss was absolutely right: I got rid of some major stresses in my life (Daria and Keith, to be exact!), and everything went back to normal.

I don't think Eileen or any of the coaches knows what happened to me. Even if Daria did tell them what she found in my drawer, they probably wouldn't have believed her. But I did think it was weird that during our group meeting this morning, Sonia started to talk about how hard it is to sustain friendships and relationships with people who weren't in the business. Maybe I'm just being paranoid. That topic of conversation could've been directed at any one of us. After all, the coaches' jobs are to prepare us for all aspects of being members of a pop band.

I for one am taking Sonia's message to heart. I'm totally swearing off men. . . at least for now!

It's so weird around here without Cass. That's kind of strange, actually, because when she lived here, she didn't seem to be around much. Her mother was always dragging her to parties, and arranging for special tutors for her. Still, I guess you don't really realize how much of a presence somebody is until they go away.

I'm glad Cass is living with her dad for a while. I think Cass's mother was the most controlling person I've ever met—and that includes my dad, who gets so frustrated when my mom and I don't obey orders the way his enlisted men do. Cass needs to know what it's like not to have follow somebody's orders all the time. Life shouldn't have to be like the military—unless that's the kind of life you choose for yourself.

I have to admit, I sometimes feel like this brownstone is a barracks. There are so many rules and schedules. I think Eileen knows I feel that way—I could tell by the way she laughed when I said, "Yes, ma'am" to her during my critique last week. She actually answered me by saying, "At ease, soldier." At least she wasn't insulted. I hadn't said it on purpose.

Anyway, in three minutes I have to be at rehearsal. So I'd better sign off now.

Alyssa

Well, the new year has started out really strangely. First Cass leaves the brownstone, and now Katie's my roommate. I don't do well with change to begin with. So you can imagine how I feel right now.

I like Katie, I really do. But I can't help feeling a little jealous of her. I mean, she's had a boyfriend her whole life, and in one afternoon she meets another guy who's crazy about her. He just picked her right out of a crowd. She may not have had the best experiences with either of those guys, but at least she knows boys notice her.

I don't get the feeling anyone's ever going to pick me out of a crowd. I'm just not that kind of girl. The only time anyone has ever noticed me is when I'm dancing. And it's not like I can just walk down Broadway doing that. Just once I'd like to know what it feels like for some boy to think I'm special.

Okay, enough with the pity party. I've got to focus on what's important right now — getting into this band. Which means, I'd better get to Sonia's vocal class, right now!

Just call me Miss Lonelyheart,

Janine

Self-Expression Journal

I'm getting that caged-in feeling again. It happens to me whenever there are too many rules in my universe. And when it comes to Eileen Kerr, rules are the name of the game. It's not just things like curfew, either. She has definite guidelines for how No Secrets songs should sound (peppy, peppy peppy), and what kind of dance moves we do (just slightly suggestive but never, ever truly sexual!). My music doesn't quite fit that mold, which is why I'm so totally afraid to let her hear her "The Bridge." I have a feeling she'll say it's not for No Secrets.

Just between you and me, I don't think Eileen Kerr's taste in music is all that great. She thinks like a businesswoman instead of an artist. It's more a case of "This will sell," or "This will never sell." It's never just "Wow, what a great tune!" I think that's what's making me nervous about this whole No Secrets thing: Even if I make the band, will I be able to deal with being a part of something I don't totally believe in?

Melanie

Self-Expression Journal

AM I THE ONLY ONE IN THIS BROWNSTONE WHO REMEMBERS WHY WE'RE HERE IN THE FIRST PLACE? I swear, everyone seems so scatterbrained these days. Hannah and Melanie are working on a song Eileen will never go for. Katie's life is like a never-ending romance soap opera. Alyssa and Janine keep whispering and giggling like this is just some sort of slumber party, and Daria spends her days playing spy, trying to get dirt on the rest of us. Don't any of them get it? We're here to hone our performance skills so that we can be part of Eileen Kerr's biggest success yet!

Well, I'm not going to remind the others of that fact anymore. I'm just going to focus on me. I want to make sure I make the band. I'm taking whatever free time I have and working on what the coaches want me to improve. Sonia says I need to make my dancing look like it comes more naturally to me. So I just keep practicing the moves again and again. I figure sooner or later they'll just become part of me. What can I say—it's all part of my good old Midwestern work ethic.

I probably shouldn't admit this, but I almost resent having to do my schoolwork. It has so little to do with being part of a band. And I hate being distracted from what's really important to me. But Eileen says we have to keep up with the girls at PCBS, so I'm doing my assignments—like writing in this notebook.

I know that some of the girls around here are getting really tight with each other, and that I'm not really part of their cliques. I've gotta admit, sometimes that hurts. But when any kind of loneliness or anything comes over me, I just try to focus on why I'm here. TO MAKE THE BAND!

Yours till Niagara falls,

Serena

Self-Expression Journal

I think I've actually made a friend. It's a very weird sensation for me. All my life I've sort of stayed away from making any friends.

It's not like Melanie and I sit up and gossip the way Alyssa and Janine do. We mostly talk about music. I think she's kinda surprised that I know as much about music as I do. But my mom's an opera freak, and even though Melanie's music is pretty far from Verdi, there are similarities in the way you can use voices as actual instruments.

I'm still very careful not to talk about my home life at all. I wouldn't want Melanie to ask too many prying questions that I can't answer. I try to talk about things that go on at the brownstone—where she and I have similar experiences. So far, that's been working pretty well. At least she hasn't called me Princess for the last three days.

Well, that's about all for now. I have to go study for my English exam tomorrow. Blech!

Hannah

P.S. No offense, Ms. Lawrence. I know you're an English teacher and all. I just hate tests.

"Oh, what do you do?" Janine asked.

Alec didn't quite know how to reply to that one. Usually, when people found out he was a Daytime Emmy Award-winning actor on the most popular soap opera in the country, their attitude towards him changed. They either tried to act cool and pretend not to care, or they cozied up to him because they were intoxicated by his fame. He didn't want either of these things to happen right now. It was far too much fun having a normal conversation with this girl. "Right now, what I do is hang out with you," he replied finally, with just a touch of mystery in his voice.

find out what happens with
Janine and Alec in...

no secrets

The Story of a Girl Band

 **Spring Fever**

by Nancy Krulik

for more information about this book,
visit our website at
www.penguinputnam.com